"So you don't want an affair?"

"No."

"What a pity!" Steven laughed. "You mightn't be tough, Bronte, but you're a great kisser." He lifted a hand and gently caressed her cheek.

"And that's the only one we're going to share together," she told him crisply.

"Don't panic. What a prickly, touchy person you are." He slid his arm companionably through hers. "It's a miracle I've warmed to you so quickly."

Margaret Way takes great pleasure in her work and works hard at her pleasure. She enjoys tearing off to the beach with her family at weekends, loves haunting galleries and auctions, and is completely given over to French champagne 'for every possible joyous occasion'. She was born and educated in the river city of Brisbane, Australia, and now lives within sight and sound of beautiful Moreton Bay.

Recent titles by the same author:

OUTBACK ANGEL
SARAH'S BABY*
RUNAWAY WIFE*
OUTBACK BRIDEGROOM*
OUTBACK SURRENDER*
HOME TO EDEN*
INNOCENT MISTRESS
HIS HEIRESS WIFE

Koomera Crossing mini-series

THE AUSTRALIAN TYCOON'S PROPOSAL

BY
MARGARET WAY

MILLS & BOON and MILLS & BOON with the Rose Device are registered trademarks of the publisher.

*First published in Great Britain 2004
Harlequin Mills & Boon Limited,
Eton House, 18-24 Paradise Road, Richmond, Surrey TW9 1SR*

© Margaret Way, Pty., Ltd 2004

ISBN 0 263 83859 5

*Set in Times Roman 10¼ on 11¼ pt.
02-1104-58562*

*Printed and bound in Spain
by Litografia Rosés, S.A., Barcelona*

CHAPTER ONE

VOLCANIC red dust puffed up under Bronte's every step. It found its way into her expensive sandals, irritating her toes and the soles of her feet. Obviously her feet had grown tender since she had last left the jungle. Grit the colour of dried blood, she thought mawkishly, coated the fine leather. But then who in their right mind wore high heeled sandals to trudge down a bush track?

"Damn!" She tottered to a stop, in the process wrenching her ankle. Moans gave way to muttered curses. She was about as irritable as she could get. What she should be wearing was lace up boots or at least a pair of running shoes. She set down her shoulder bag that had cost an arm and a leg. Never featherlight even when empty it had been growing heavier at every step. Her small suitcase followed. It weighed over a ton. Now she was able to shake the dust and grit first from the sole of one foot, then the other.

Ah, the relief! She gulped in hot scented air.

One of her bra straps had slipped off her shoulder. She fixed that. Her sunglasses needed propping back up her nose, a water slide of sweat. She was wearing a big wide-brimmed hat, yet the blazing tropical sun was burning a hole through the top of her head. Boiling and bothered she yanked at her designer label tank top. It was wet under the arms and glued to her back. She just knew her face was the colour of a ripe plum.

"No wonder you're so darned unhappy. You're a fool, Bronte." She often talked to herself. She'd grown into that habit as a lonely and isolated little girl. She'd even had imaginary friends. Great friends they were, too. There was a girl called Em who grew along with her. A boy called Jonty who

5

was a very gentle person and lived in the rain forest. Once Gilly claimed she saw Em and Jonty playing tag around a giant strangler fig. Gilly always spoke to her as if she were an equal even when she was *seven!* Of course Gilly was having a little joke. Bronte knew her friends existed only in her powerful imagination.

A whirlwind of dust blew up, rousing her to move off the track until it passed. It was her own fault that she had to walk. Death before dishonour was her motto. She was stuck with it. She hadn't learned it. It had been passed out at birth. It got her into a lot of trouble, that's all.

It wasn't right for the taxi driver to call Great-Aunt Gillian with a hard G "a crazy old bat!" accompanied by hoots of laughter she was expected to join in. That had made her hopping mad. Not that Gilly of the copious snow-white hair, once blue-black like her own, black eyes and wicked grin didn't communicate with their dead ancestors on a regular basis. As an imaginative child Bronte, actively encouraged in her psychic powers by Gilly, had sensed long dead members of the McAllister family hanging around the place. They spent their time wandering the old sugar plantation and the big patch of virgin rain forest bordering McAllister land. They'd even been seen up on the main road, scaring the tourists. The locals took no notice whatsoever.

Gilly, despite her solitary, secluded life, was right up there as a local character in an area that was legendary for its "characters." Gilly was the Bush Medicine Woman. The plantation, the two hundred acres that remained from the original selection, would attract a lot of developers if it were ever put on the market, but Gilly lived a frugal life. Most of her inherited money had gone. "I've lived too long!" She supplemented what was left, by running a profitable little side-line selling herbal potions, concoctions, the odd aphrodisiac—said to work—facial and body creams guaranteed to alleviate the symptoms of every discomfort known to woman including the "infernal itches". Gilly having been stood up at the altar fifty odd years ago didn't give a hang what happened to the men. They could look after themselves.

Bronte didn't love men either. She was amazed anyone did! Most of them turned out to be bitter disappointments. Not that she'd been stuck on her lonesome in front of the altar. She was the one who found commitment darn near impossible. To prove it, with one week to the Big Day, she'd recently called off her much publicised society wedding, bringing her mother's and her demented stepfather's fury down on her head. She'd made a fool of them but she had learned that she was a fool already. Her actions, apparently, put her on a par with some sort of a criminal. A mass swindler perhaps? The humiliation was not to be borne. The disgrace! Worse, it was bad for business.

Nat, her fiancé, had been angry enough to call her names, grinding his teeth as he did so. He wore not so much a devastated as totally baffled expression. What girl in her right mind would give *him* up? A girl could get tramped to death standing in line to meet Nathan Saunders.

Nat's mother had been livid! In fact she'd been astoundingly crude. Bronte hadn't realized Nat's mother *knew* let alone *used* four letter words. "No breeding!" sniffed Gilly when she heard. Nothing like scorning a son to bring out the worst in a mother. No one stood up Thea Saunders's—one of society's leading lights—wonder boy. She had demanded the 3 carat diamond solitaire back, not that Bronte had ever intended to keep it. Her finger felt a whole lot lighter without it. Bronte had consoled herself with the knowledge that she wasn't the first girl to have second thoughts about tying the knot. The big problem was she hadn't been able to work up the courage to voice her concerns until the last minute. Pathetic really! For that, she despised herself but she knew the turbulence her decision would create.

Turbulence. Chaos. A tongue-lashing from the stepfather she detested. Nat had been hand-picked for her. She was ashamed to admit she was still trying to please her mother when let's be straight about it, she never had. Her rejection of Nat Saunders had caused a huge scandal. Few of her so-called friends had sided with her. She was scolded and marvelled at at every turn. She had everything going for her and she blew it! What an idiot! The word had become an alternative to fool. Her mother had ended most sentences with one or the other.

The handsome and popular Nat was the scion of media mogul Richard Saunders, a close friend and partner in various enterprises—probably dodgy—of her stepfather Carl Brandt. Of course she lost her budding career. A swift retribution that did nothing to raise her spirits. Over the past year she'd swum into the limelight as a popular character in the award winning TV police drama *Shadows*. Two weeks ago she had met with a very bloody end. A shoot-out. Officer down. It had blitzed the ratings and caused a storm of protests from her fans—she never knew she had so many—but she wasn't going to be allowed to get away with shaming two outstandingly rich families.

Her mother had given her hell, like it was her main aim in life to make Bronte's existence intolerable.

"How can any of us hold up our heads?" Miranda had exploded. "After all Carl has done for you, you ungrateful little *fool!*"

What exactly *had* Carl done for her? He hadn't adopted her. Her own father had left her enough money to cover her education through university, pay for her upkeep and her clothes. Her mother still beautiful and sexy at forty-five—never mind she had celebrated that birthday twice already—had not been her first husband's beneficiary. Bronte had been that, her inheritance administered by her late father's lawyer as executor of his will. Apparently Ross McAllister hadn't trusted his wife to do that. Bronte found out years later her father had changed his will on the very day of his death. Her mother had got away with the family home, all the contents and her cache of jewellery, a veritable Aladdin's Cave, otherwise she'd been cut out entirely. There was a story there, with in all probability grave implications, but nothing could bring her father back. She had loved him so much! She could still feel his hand patting the top of her head.

Her remarried mother sided with her new husband on everything. Perhaps she had no alternative? Bronte understood it was easier on her mother that way. Carl Brandt was a big shouldered, imposing looking man with heavy lidded, obsidian eyes and a very loud voice. No one would ever have to ask her stepfather to repeat himself. Yet for reasons totally beyond Bronte, her stepfather was positively *magnetic* to women who liked a touch of the brute. On the proviso, of course, he was powerful and had lots of money. Even age didn't seem to come into it. Such men retained their attractions at over ninety unlike women who some believed started the downhill slide once they hit thirty.

Her mother had always been attracted to money and power. Never mind that Carl Brandt was a tyrant, with a tongue like a chain saw. Bronte's own gentlemanly father had doted on her but he had been taken from her when she was only seven. Killed when his high powered sports car crashed into a tree. Her mother thereafter maintained Ross McAllister was a reckless driver with a thirst for speed. An opinion rejected by his many friends.

Bronte's life had changed dramatically after that. Her mother had acted deranged for a couple of days, a tragic figure on the verge of a breakdown. Bronte had been sent to live with her maternal grandparents, an arrangement that lasted only a few months. Her grandmother—not the kindest granny in the world—decided she couldn't tolerate Bronte's "tantrums" any longer. Children should be seen, but not heard whereas Bronte had been given to creating disturbances. That's when Gilly McAllister had come to the rescue. Gilly had offered to look after her. Good old "crazy" Gilly. Thank goodness for her! Gilly who privately called Miranda "shallow and egotistical." Bronte was meant to stay with her great-aunt until Miranda felt more able to cope after her tragic loss.

Bronte stayed *five* years. She saw her mother rarely. As her husband's *property*—Brandt owned people—Miranda had to be on hand at all times. Her grandmother she saw not at all. "I can't believe our luck!" Gilly chortled. Neither of them were asked to Miranda's and Brandt's society wedding which took place an unseemly month or so after Ross McAllister's tragic death. So much for the tragedy queen and the nervous breakdown that never was. Then again, perhaps it illustrated Miranda's extraordinary resilience.

A suspiciously short period of time later Bronte's half brother Max—poor little victimised Max—made his much gossiped about entry into the world though Bronte and Gilly locked away in the deep Far North didn't get to hear about that happy event until at least a year later when Gilly read about Max's existence in the newspaper.

On her twelfth birthday Bronte's mother—no one saw it coming—made the decision to send Bronte to an exclusive boarding school back in Sydney. "We have to get you away from this primitive place!" Miranda had cried, accelerating away from the plantation so fast she sent up a dust storm. "You're nothing but a savage. I was a fool to let Gilly look after you. She can't even look after herself." Miranda had appeared genuinely shocked at the run-down condition of the old plantation gone back to jungle and Bronte's appearance which even Bronte had to admit in retrospect must have been a little on the wild side. With Gilly for a mentor Bronte had gotten used to wearing a sort of safari outfit—boy's shirts and trousers with a thick belt and good stout boots. She'd have worn that outfit to school, where she shone academically, only the headmistress, Miss Prentice, wouldn't have let her through the front gate.

The day Bronte left, her darling Gilly had cried, her tall, vigorous body bent over and shaking like she had a tropical fever.

Gilly who was as brave and fierce as the general in the family. General Alexander "Sandy" McAllister who'd risen to fame in India fighting for the British in the Afghan wars. "Sandy" was one of Gilly's favourites from the family spirit world. After his long stint in India Sandy's spirit had settled in well to the humid heat of the rain forest, unfazed by the cyclones that blew in from time to time.

Feeling a little rested Bronte slung her bag back over her shoulder then picked up her expensive suitcase. It was one of her mother's discards. Her mother enjoyed enormously being the wife of a very rich man. Rich men ran the world! Wealth defined the man! Brandt pampered her mother for a good reason. Miranda was always on show as his wife. Her beauty and elegance were legendary and she had a wonderful flair for dressing. Why else would Brandt have married her? It all reflected wonderfully well on his taste.

Otherwise he was far from being a generous man. He had never been generous to Bronte. She would have been walking around in rags, uneducated, if not for the inheritance her own darling father had left her. Her mother didn't believe in spoiling her either. Worse Brandt was downright mean to his own son. Poor Max who hadn't inherited any of his father's abominable skills and bully boy nature. The endless criticisms, the cutting sarcasm, the scorn the two of them had endured. It had been tough to leave fifteen-year-old Max behind, but at least Max had respite at boarding school. He'd even dug in his heels to stay at school through vacations. Something that had affronted their mother who laboured under the monstrous delusion she was a good mother.

My sad, dysfunctional family! Bronte thought. There was a crisis every day of the week. She was always amazed she could look so much like her mother yet be nothing like her in her nature and behaviour. It was Gilly who had taught her values, shown her love and understanding. Gilly was the woman of substance not her own mother whom she continued to love even as she despaired of ever having her love returned. Beautiful Miranda who at the drop of a hat—for instance a broken engagement—could turn into a shrieking virago. If Brandt was famous for his lung power, he could on occasion be equalled by her mother.

Bronte staggered on bravely, remembering how Gilly had always called her "plucky." As a child it had made her laugh. *Plucky.* For some reason—the obvious clucky—she associated it with Gilly's chooks. Despite Bronte's multiple discomforts she was drinking in her surroundings. She loved this place. It was the Garden of Eden complete with the snakes. The countryside was glorious. The coastal corridor north of Capricorn was as lush and bountiful as the Interior across the Great Divide was arid. She adored the rampant blossoming of the tropics. The brilliantly plumaged birds. The colour!

Bougainvillea ran like wildfire on either side of the private track. You could hardly call it a road. It was near impassable in heavy rains. The magnificent parasite covered fences, climbed trees, old water tanks. Orange. Cerise. Scarlet. Pink. Blue-violet morning glories "the colour of your eyes, Bronte" Gilly had told her as a child, cascaded over the sides of one of those old water tanks that stood in an abandoned field.

Once these fields had been under sugar, at maturity towering higher than a man, but production had stopped on Oriole long before she'd been born and Gilly had inherited the old plantation that once had been a prolific money spinner. McAllister land bordered onto the gallery rain forest where the Yellow Orioles built their deep nests and sent their incessant choom-chalooms floating sheer across the forest. It was after these rain forest birds the plantation had been named in the late 1880s.

Once I knew this land like the back of my hand, Bronte thought. Gilly had taken her everywhere with her. Into the forest where she found the magical ingredients for her potions, to the river that had "salties" in it, big man-eating estuarine crocodiles, to the beautiful beaches with their white sand and turquoise waters, to the islands of one of the great wonders of the natural world, The Great Barrier Reef where they'd gone swimming and snorkelling and exploring the coral. Gilly had taught her to ride a horse—"you just hold on, Bronte! Show 'im who's boss." How to handle a .22 rifle. "Just in case!" Bronte really hoped Gilly had turned in her guns. She wouldn't put it past her to have hidden one beneath the floor boards.

"By the time I reach the homestead I'll be a wreck," Bronte grumbled to herself. "Ready to throw myself head first into the lily lagoon, maybe cavort naked." There was never anyone around. The homestead was at the far end of the track. She could see the tall vine-bedecked wall around the home grounds. The massive wrought-iron gates bore an elaborately scrolled Oriole picked out in bronze. Gilly wouldn't be home until late. She had an appointment with a visiting eye specialist at the town clinic. Bronte worried about that. Was Gilly's wonderful eyesight failing despite her disclaimers? Such things happened with age. Who needed to get old? Bronte had refused to let Gilly cancel her appointment. She wouldn't get another for at least six weeks.

"A bad day, lovey, for me to have to go."

Bronte had soothed her great-aunt by saying she'd catch a cab from the train station. She'd flown from Sydney to Brisbane, but decided to take "The Queenslander" north instead of continuing by air. She wanted a long time to *think*. The train was great for that. It was a long scenic trip through increasingly beautiful country as one crossed the Tropic of Capricorn. The Queenslander was comfortable. They served lovely meals and the sleeping arrangements were excellent. Lots of gazing out the window. Of course she'd fully expected to be dropped at the door until that crack about the "old bat!" She couldn't let anyone get away with saying that about Gilly.

A bead of perspiration trickled into her eyes. It stung.

"Damn!" She dropped the suitcase so she could shove her straw hat further down on her head.

It was then she became aware of a car engine. She turned in time to see a vehicle turn off the bitumen road and head down Oriole's private track.

Gilly! Her lifesaver! Wouldn't she give her a great big hug! But why so early?

Bronte stood quite still, watching the 4WD approaching in a cloud of red dust. The problem was, Gilly didn't have a 4WD. As far as she knew, Gilly still drove an ancient utility that had never broken down in twenty years. All Gilly ever had to do was kick the tyres. The 4WD was coming straight for her, insisting on right of way. Could you beat that? She was a McAllister. She wasn't about to get off her own road. This would be her place when her darling Gilly was gone. She'd live up here and turn into a feisty self-sufficient medicine woman, like her great-aunt. Historically there had always been such women.

The driver of the vehicle, seeing her standing so confrontationally in the middle of the road, had the sense to detour onto the thick grassy verge. It was a godsend because the red dust settled before it could envelop her. Was it deliberate? Could the driver be considerate? On rainy days in the city as a pedestrian waiting at the lights she'd often been splashed by inconsiderate drivers who perversely picked up speed instead of slowing down in the grey conditions.

The driver was a man. A young man which greatly surprised her. What was he doing on McAllister land? Especially when Gilly wasn't at home. In that instant Bronte thought of Gilly's .22. For all she knew this man could be dangerous, on the run from the police. He was certainly trespassing and the plantation was very isolated. Bronte planted her sandalled feet with their ridiculous high heels firmly on the track. She was determined not to budge even if her self-esteem was stretched to twanging point.

Straighten your back, Bronte. Look right at him. Men

*sensed natural born victims. She'd learned that from life with
her horrible stepfather.*

The driver swung out of the vehicle, loping around the
bonnet. Bronte watched him like she'd watch an approaching
tiger.

Twenty-eight, maybe thirty. He was tall; a good six-two.
Wide in the shoulders. Lean. A splendid body really. He had
to be a fitness freak. He wore the kind of gear she used to
wear herself. Jungle greens. A crocodile hunter, maybe? Even
at a distance she noted the green, *green* eyes. His skin was
a tawny gold. He looked just the sort of guy who could handle himself anywhere, anytime. Boldly, aggressively *male*.
The sort of guy who considered male domination the natural
order. He probably had a grip to fracture her hand.

He was also devilishly handsome. She wasn't so blinded
by the sweat in her eyes, she couldn't see that. Straight nose,
high cheekbones, curly mouth, determined jaw. If she'd been
more impressionable she'd have fainted. As it was every in-
stinct shrieked a warning. She stood ramrod straight even
when her back was breaking. Her antagonism to the dominant
male was deeply entrenched. It was one reason she had taken
up with Nat, who, at bottom, was as soft as a marshmallow.

"Hi there!" Action Man's smile was so warm and friendly
it took her aback. That smile lit up his entire face.

Bronte stared in disbelief. She didn't reply. She waited for
him to come up to her, frowning darkly just in case he got
any ideas.

"Steven Randolph. I'm a friend of your great-aunt's." He
introduced himself, taking in every detail of her overheated
appearance. Little sparks seemed to be flying around her
tallish delicate frame.

Bronte stood her ground. Height was one of the assets
Mother Nature had bestowed on her. His voice, at least, was
something in her favour. It wasn't *loud*. In fact it was smooth
and mellow. Most women would find it a real turn-on. It
struck her it was also the voice of money and education. His

stance wasn't arrogant, more an elegant slouch. There was no doubting he was very comfortable in his own skin.

"I know the names of my great-aunt's friends," she said, as coolly as she could in the blistering heat. "I've never heard of a Steven Randolph."

"Perhaps Gilly was waiting to surprise you," he suggested and smiled as though amused by her antagonism. Very white teeth. Straight. Strong. Why was he making her so *angry?* He was trying to be pleasant, while she was bristling like a porcupine.

"You're Bronte, aren't you." It was a statement not a question.

"Congratulations." It suddenly struck Bronte her stepfather's abrasive manner might have brushed off on her. How terribly distressing!

Another smile. An engaging quirk of the mouth. "Gilly has photographs of you all over the house. Occasionally I even got to see you on the television. Very good you were, too. The shoot-out nearly broke my heart."

Bronte winced. "Can we leave my ex-career out of the conversation?"

"Certainly. Could I say first what they did to you was rough. I expect you don't want to talk about your broken engagement, either?"

She shielded her eyes with her hand. She was getting a crick in the neck just looking up at him despite her own height. "Are you trying to be cruel or does it just come naturally?"

He appeared surprised. "I thought you were the one to opt out. Did I get that wrong? If I did, I'm very sorry."

"You're not sorry at all," she fired up.

"Of course I am. I'm not sorry for Saunders not that you'd have made him the perfect wife."

Bronte almost choked. "Really? How can you tell?"

"I know of the family. You *wouldn't* want to move in with them."

Bronte frowned at him fiercely. "Thanks for the tip but you're already too late. Anyway, I can save you a trip. Gilly isn't home."

"I know that, she's at the eye specialist. I've brought her supplies home. They're in the car. You look hot. You really ought to get out of the sun. What are you doing walking anyway? And in those high heels!" He all but clicked his tongue.

"I like the exercise," she snapped.

Suddenly his demeanour changed from friendly to grim. "Don't tell me the taxi driver left you at the road? Who was it? Describe him."

"So you can beat him to a pulp?" she only half joked.

"Why ever would you say that? I can get my message across without violence. *Please*. Get into the car. I'll drive you up to the house. Let me take your things."

She wanted to be in the position to ignore him but sad to say she wasn't. She had the feeling he wouldn't take any notice anyway. Already he had her heavy suitcase in hand, stowing it in the back of the vehicle like it was a paper bag.

"Come along," he coaxed. "Much more of this and you'd be badly sunburnt."

"I don't burn," she told him, when she was seated in the vehicle and he was driving back onto the track. "I have olive skin. I spent years up here."

"I know." He grinned. "Bronte on horseback. Bronte feeding a joey that had lost its mother. Bronte holding a rifle of all things. You must have been ten?" He gave her a half amused half disproving glance. "Bronte in the rain forest amid the ferns. Bronte at speech night where she collected all the prizes."

"Why would you bother to look at old photographs of me?" The air-conditioning was heaven! She closed her eyes briefly and arched her neck.

"They were kinda cute actually." He allowed his eyes to rest on her. She was even more beautiful, more *sensuous* in the flesh than she was on television. And those eyes! What colour were they? The lilac-blue of the sacred lotus? The morning glories that decked Oriole's fences? A crush of jacaranda blossom? "Gilly adores you," he said.

"I adore Gilly." She answered with a touch of belligerence as if he'd expressed doubts about her affection. "I would never have survived without her." Immediately she made it she regretted the confidence.

"That's a sad thing to say." His voice, however, conveyed only empathy and genuine concern.

She didn't need it. "I'm sorry I said it."

"What is it about me you don't like?" he asked, sounding like he wanted to get to the bottom of her antagonism.

Arrogant beast to keep challenging her! "I'm sure I have no opinion of you at all," she lied. She'd been accumulating data from the instant she set eyes on him.

"Good grief! What will Gilly say when you tell her you can't stand the sight of me. Do I remind you of someone?"

She felt her cheeks grow hotter with resentment. "Forgive me if I'm being rude." She made a huge effort to get hold of herself. "It's the heat."

Her lovely skin was dewed with sweat. He found it incredibly erotic. He could see the tips of her nipples budded against her tight tank top with its low oval neck. A tiny trickle of sweat ran down between her breasts. Her yellow stretch jeans printed with flowers showed the length of her legs. "I thought you loved it?" he asked lazily.

"Not when I'm carrying a suitcase."

"So the taxi driver offended you?"

"Determined to work this out?" She shot a quick glance at him. Bronte had never cared for cleft chins, and she hardened her heart against him to be on the safe side.

"Oddly enough I am." He met her gaze with a slightly puzzled expression. She was being rather awful. His clear green eyes moved over her face and shoulders. It was a glance that didn't linger. It wasn't overtly *sexual* yet she felt a rush of something powerfully like sexual excitement. It would be the greatest folly to allow him to see it. A guy like that would only exploit the situation.

"I reacted—perhaps overreacted—to one of his remarks. He called Gilly a crazy old bat. When I think about it, it was more indulgent than anything. You know, the local character!"

"Are you *sure?*"

"I'm sure I don't want you to go after him. What do you do around here, Mr. Randolph?"

"Steven, please," he pleaded, mockery in his voice. "Steve if you like. Gilly calls me Steven. I'm a developer of sorts."

She almost hunkered down in her seat. "Not one of those!"

He gave a short laugh. "I don't go around destroying the environment, Bronte. I'm a conservationist as well as a developer."

Her expression was highly sceptical. "I thought they were mutually exclusive. I can't imagine how you got to be friendly with Gilly who's been a conservationist all her life. Unless she has something you want?"

"And what would that be?" He flashed a glance at her.

He wasn't supposed to have that sexy a voice, she thought irritably. Wives might leave their husbands for a voice like that. "Oriole, maybe?" she suggested. "It might be run-down but these days with a thriving tourist industry and so close to the Reef it's become a very valuable parcel of land. You might like to get it rezoned and put a back-packer's place on it for all I know. I should put you straight. Gilly has left it to me."

"I *know!*" He dragged the word out. "You must love her for it?"

She ignored the sarcasm. "Gilly told you *that?*" The fact Gilly liked this guy threw her off-balance. Okay he had charisma. Was that enough to make Gilly confide so much? He'd taken his akubra off, throwing it on the back seat where it appeared to be cuddling up to her straw hat. His hair was a dark mahogany colour with copper highlights put in by the sun. It was thick, straight, well behaved hair. A touch too full and long, but sexy.

"You'd be surprised how much Gilly and I talk." He confirmed her worst fears.

"No kidding! Like I said, she's never mentioned you."

"Well, you have had a great deal on your mind. If it's any consolation, you did the right thing. If I were a girl I wouldn't marry Nat Saunders, either. Not in a million years!"

"It sounds more like you *know* him rather than know of him. Do you?" It wasn't impossible.

"Kind of." He grinned.

"More like you're having me on," Bronte snapped.

He didn't deny it.

They were driving through Oriole's open gates. "Someone's fixed the hinge, that's good," she mumbled to herself. The last time she'd visited Gilly which had to be six or seven months ago, the sagging left side of the gate was propped back with a brick.

"I come in handy sometimes," he said.

Bronte scarcely heard him. She was staring about her in amazement. "Good grief, a huge clean-up has gone on since I was last here!" The jungle that had threatened to engulf the entire plantation as well as devour the timber homestead had been slashed right back. A good section was actually *mown!* "Amazing!" She stared out at the grounds which even under jungle were so wildly beautiful they took the breath away.

The gravelled driveway, flanked by an avenue of magnificent poincianas formed a broad highway up to the plantation house. The branches of the great shade trees had grown so massive they interlocked in the middle, forming a long cool tunnel leading up to the house. In a month or so they would burst into glorious flower. An unforgettable sight!

Ancient fig trees on her left. *Giants!* Festooned with huge staghorns and elkhorns grown as epiphytes, climbing orchids with strongly scented cascading sprays of white and yellow; lacey ferns. One of the rain forest figs she had named Ludwig as a child—after the famous early explorer Ludwig Leichardt—had fourteen foot high buttresses. When she had first come here Gilly had cleaned them out so she could use Ludwig for a cubby house. The greatest miracle of all was she had never been bitten by a snake though she had seen plenty and took good care to tread carefully.

On her right were the magnolias and palms galore. Fan palms with fronds four feet across. There were always shrubs blooming; oleander, frangipani, hibiscus, gardenia, tibouchina, Rain of Gold, the colourful pentas grown en masse, as were the great clumping beds of strelitzias—Bird of Paradise, and the agapanthus. The unbelievably fragrant but poisonous daturas, called the Angel's Trumpets, were in flower, the enormous white trumpets dangling freely from the branches.

Through the trees she could see the dark emerald waters of the lily pond. A lagoon really, a natural spring. Dozens of glistening cup-like sacred lotus and their pads decorated the glassy surface. A small sturdy bridge had been built across the pond many years ago. Now the latticed sides hung with a delphinium-blue vine, the long trails of flowers dipping down to the water.

The banks of flowering lantana hadn't been touched. The pink lantana attracted the butterflies, gorgeous specimens, lacewings, birdwings, cruisers, spotted triangles, the glorious iridescent blue Ulysses. They flew around the great sprawling masses of tiny clustered flowers, wings beating in a brilliant kaleidoscope of colour. In the back garden grew every tropical fruit known to man. Mangoes, paw-paws, bananas, loquats, guavas, passionfruit, custard apples, and all the citrus fruits, too, lemons, limes, mandarins, grapefruit, cumquats. There was even a grove of macadamias, the now native

Queensland nut transported from Hawaii by an enterprising businessman.

"I love this place," she breathed. "It's always been my sanctuary."

He glanced at her, taking in her dreamy expression. "We all need a sanctuary at certain times. Otherwise we have to get out there into the world."

Her mood was broken. "Are you implying Gilly didn't?"

"I was thinking more of *you*."

"I don't follow."

"Don't sound so cross," he answered. "It just struck me in passing you might be harbouring thoughts of turning into a recluse."

"I prefer to think of it as finding a life of Zen-like purity and simplicity."

Bronte turned her head away pointedly.

"You're a bit young for that yet," he said. "Solitude is great from time to time, but there are hardships associated with living in isolation."

"I'll bear that in mind."

The driveway opened out into a wide circle that enclosed a very charming three-tiered fountain, the largest bowl supported by four swans. The fountain had been out of action for years, now it was actually playing. "Have we *you* to thank for the massive clean-up?" She didn't sound at all grateful and was rather ashamed of the fact. But she intended to stick to her guns.

"I feel better if I can do a good deed now and then," he said. "I told you, Gilly is my friend. She's remarkably sprightly but she's seventy-six years old."

Was that a dig? "No need to remind me. Did she pay you?"

His green gaze was lancing. "I *told* you, it was a good deed."

"You mean it was a big project." It must have taken weeks, even months.

"So? I could handle it. Are we going to get out? You first. I'll follow."

Ordering her around already. In the act of opening the door Bronte turned back sharply. "Are you coming in?"

"Fear not," he mocked. "It's only for a short time, I have Gilly's provisions in the back. Cold stuff in the esky that needs to go into the fridge. I thought I told you?"

"I have a short attention span, I'm afraid," she announced haughtily, standing out on the drive where her toes suffered another assault from the gravel. She stared up at the house. A green and white timber mansion. Of course it had been built for a large prominent family who had loved entertaining. These days its upkeep was a monstrous burden to Gilly though she'd rather die than admit it. The house was perched a few feet off the ground on capped stumps, a deterrent to the white ants. In her childhood one could scarcely tell where the jungle finished and the homestead started. Today the old colonial was revealed in all its enchantment.

Low set, with verandahs on three sides, twin bow windows flanked the front door. Their position was matched by the hips on the corrugated iron roof. The verandahs were enclosed by particularly fine white wrought-iron lace visible at long last because the rampant creepers that had obscured it for many years had been stripped off. The house had been recently repainted its original glossy white. The iron roof had been restored to a harmonious green matching the shutters on the French doors.

"Your work, too, no doubt?" She turned her head over her shoulder to where Action Man was unloading the 4WD.

"Like it?"

"I love it!" she muttered. "Either you're a philanthropist on the grand scale or you have an ulterior motive."

"Believe as you will, Bronte." He shrugged as if he didn't care a jot.

Picturesque as the homestead undoubtedly was, what made it so unique was the spectacular setting. In the background, on McAllister land was the unobstructed view of an emerald shrouded volcanic plug. It rose in a cone-shaped peak with a single curiously shaped hump. Gilly had always called it Rex as in Dinosaurus Rex. Rex stood sentinel over the house. The peak wasn't high, only around four hundred feet but it looked magical against the peacock-blue sky.

"If you're finished admiring your inheritance you might like to take a box or two," he called. "Some of them aren't heavy."

"Let me get these sandals off first," she responded tartly. "They looked great when I first set out. Now they're killing me."

He carried the bulk of the provisions in and he wasn't even puffing. Sometimes it must be good to be a man. There were quite a lot of cardboard boxes. Obviously Gilly had stocked up for her visit. She never did remember Bronte didn't eat nearly as much as she used to as a child when she'd been unfillable. Not that she'd ever put on an extra ounce. Of course as a child she'd been in touch with her legs. The modern child rode in cars and sat cross-legged in front of the television. She and Gilly had tramped the forest. Every morning, except in the rain, she had walked the track to catch the school bus. Every afternoon the bus driver left her at the same spot.

Yes, she was ideally suited to a Spartan existence.

"So, why don't you freshen up while I put these away?" he suggested.

What a cheek! She swept her long wavy hair off her nape. "Go to the devil!"

He raised a mocking brow. "Do you mind! You're a prickly little thing, aren't you? Not a bit like our Gilly."

"I'm not *little* at all," she flashed. "And she's not your Gilly. I just look little beside you. What are you, six-six?"

"Not even in high heeled boots. It's a good thing you're not in search of another husband, Bronte."

More insults. "You don't think I could get one?" She was amazed to see a man in Gilly's kitchen. A man so at *home* there.

"Easily, for the pleasure of *looking* at you. But..."

She bristled at what he left unsaid. "Well, *you* don't have to worry. Or are you married?"

"Married, no. But I've been Best Man." His eyes swept over her. The high-bred face, so touchingly haughty, the delicate height, the silky masses of her long hair, curling up in the heat, the wonderful colouring. "I'm a committed bachelor at the moment. I have to notch up a few achievements before I'm ready to ask a woman to marry me."

"Really?" She raised her brows. "I'm surprised you haven't lots of achievements under your belt already?" The odd part, she actually *was*.

"I'm sorry the answer's no. I have a law degree. Not much else."

"Then why aren't you practising?"

"I can make a lot more money as an entrepreneur," he said bluntly.

She found herself pulling a face. "I *hate* men whose main aim in life is to make money. Seeing you're so entrepreneurial you might like to make me a cup of tea. Much as I love Gilly I can't drink her home grown, home roasted coffee. It tastes like the mud at the bottom of the lily pond. By the way, you shouldn't take the eggs out of the carton. *In* the carton is the best way to store them not in the egg rack. What happened to Gilly's chooks?"

He gave a surprisingly graceful shrug of his wide shoulders. "The things one learns!" He started to put the eggs back in the cardboard carton. "The chooks didn't have much of a show with the snakes. Especially with the chook house fallen down. That's one of the reasons I and my trusty workers got stuck into cleaning up the grounds.''

"You're a saint!" said Bronte, giving him a little salute before disappearing down the hallway. "Saint Stephen. I can't remember what happened to *him.*''

CHAPTER TWO

"WHAT did you think of Steven?" Gilly asked, looking with the greatest interest into Bronte's face.

"What was I supposed to think of him?" Bronte parried, deadpan.

"*Tell* me, you little tease!" Gilly seized her hand. They were sitting in the kitchen over a cup of coffee. Gilly had only been home ten minutes, most of the conversation taken up with Gilly's visit to the eye specialist. The problem could not be cured but thank goodness it was manageable. "Not as nice as mine!" Gilly sniffed critically at the rich fragrant brew beneath her slightly hooked nose.

Bronte had to laugh. "Which says a lot for your cast-iron stomach. Actually they're very good Italian beans. I put them through the grinder."

"I expect Steven was thinking of you," Gilly said, quite fondly for a woman usually incapable of finding a good word for a man. "I must have told him you didn't like your coffee as full bodied as my home grown roast. He's nothing if not thoughtful."

Bronte set down her near empty cup, with a feeling of astonishment. She stared into Gilly's much loved face. It was seamed, the skin tanned to the texture of soft leather, stretched tight over the prominent cheek bones. Gilly's eyebrows were still pitch-black making a piquant contrast to the abundant snow-white hair she had always worn in a thick loose bun. It was a very much out of the ordinary face, Bronte decided. "In love with him, are you?" she jibed.

Gilly responded with an unexpected sigh. "I'm ever so slowly realizing I could have wasted my life, Bronte, girl.

Just because I burnt my fingers once, I shouldn't have let it put me off men for good.''

"Gosh I thought you loved being a recluse," Bronte looked at her great-aunt with as much surprise as if she had just expressed regret at not reaching the summit of Everest. "Why, you're *famous* around here."

"And I deserve to be. Every bit!" Gilly harrumphed. "Didn't I clear up Hetty Bannister's terrible leg ulcers when her doctor couldn't? I've cured dozens of cases of psoriasis, eczema, rosacea, you name it, over the years. I've got a home remedy for everything.'' Gilly leaned down to whack a mosquito that had the temerity to land on her ankle. "I hope you're not interested in becoming a recluse yourself?"

Bronte grimaced. "I might have to, seeing I dumped the love of my life a week from the altar.''

"You're not regretting it, are you, lovie?" Gilly's black eyes sharpened over Bronte's face. She was wearing new lenses in her old spectacle frames. Now she re-adjusted them on her nose.

"I'm regretting I was nuts enough to get mixed up with him in the first place," Bronte confessed.

Gilly looked at her great-niece with loving sympathy. "That was your mother pushing you every step of the way. It was a wonder you didn't have a breakdown. You always end up trying to please her.''

"She *is* my mother," Bronte put her elbows on the table, resting her face in her hands. "You're my fairy godmother. I don't know what I'd do without you, Gilly. You're my haven.''

"You bet your life I am!" Gilly frowned ferociously. "It's not as though you were going to marry Prince Charming anyway. You can't be too upset about it?"

"Gilly, I've had hell," Bronte said simply. "I vow here and now I can't go through it again. I've had to listen to Miranda's rages—'' Miranda had long since banned the word *Mum* "—then Carl's, sometimes both together. It was like

the start of World War III. A woman is a fool to marry for
love, Miranda told me. A woman should marry for *security*."

"And wasn't she just the girl to arrange it. Though they
do use the two words together," Gilly attempted to be fair.
"Marriage. Security. I think you were very brave getting out
in time. The suicide rate is high enough!"

"You were telling me the truth about your eyes?" Bronte
changed the subject to one of more pressing interest to her.
She was sick to death of her own traumas.

"'Course I was," Gilly said, sitting so upright her back
was straight as a crowbar. "Routine pressure check for glaucoma. No sign of it. Glaucoma is hereditary anyway and
there's no family history as far as I know. I get a few flashing
lights in my right eye, but nothing to worry about. Like I
told you it's manageable. I'll see him every six months. All
in all I'm a fit old girl with a strong constitution. The sort of
person who lives to be one hundred, not that I want to last
that long, the only way to go is down. Why don't we take a
stroll before sunset. Steven has worked wonders. I'm darn
happy with that young man."

"So I see!" Bronte despised herself for feeling jealous.
"Surely he couldn't have done it all for *nothing?* It would
have been a very big job. He told me he had workers?"

"They're from the croc farm," Gilly announced casually
over her shoulder, leading the way out onto the verandah.

"Croc farm? *Croc farm!*" Bronte shuddered. "What are
you saying, Gilly? He doesn't have a croc farm, does he?"

"It was a real smart business move if you ask me," Gilly
said, stomping down the short flight of steps. "The tourists
love the crocs and the reptiles, especially the Japanese. Our
world famous crocodile man is moving his whole operation
closer to Brisbane. Chika Moran has been doing very nicely
for years with Wildwood but he lost a partner as you know."

"To a crocodile, I believe."

"I guess he prodded that old croc one time too many,"
Gilly said. "Anyway Steven's not in on that side of it."

"Thank goodness!" Bronte put a hand over her breast. Used to the sight of crocodiles for years of her life they still frightened the living daylights out of her.

"Steven will handle the business side," Gilly said, waving a scented gardenia beneath her nose. "He knows all about environmental issues, and he's good with people."

"What is he, *insane?*" Bronte asked sarcastically.

"What do you mean, love?" Gilly halted so abruptly, Bronte all but slammed into her. "Steven isn't about to arm wrestle the crocs, if that's what you're worried about. I told you he won't be involved with that side of the business at all. He and Chika are considering expanding into a kind of zoo. There's big money in it."

"Like a few lions and tigers, a giraffe or two?" Bronte suggested in the same sarcastic vein. "Elephants are obligatory. Everyone loves elephants. A rhino would be nice. I believe in Africa rhinos happily consort with crocodiles. There's a thought! Did you know *white* rhino is a misnomer. It was originally *wide* referring to the size of their mouths which are bigger than the black rhino, though who got to measure their lips I can't imagine. A bit of trivia for you."

"That's interesting." Gilly smiled on her much as she had when Bronte, the great reader, had come up with a piece of unusual information as a child. "Anyway Chika has the land to make the idea of a zoo feasible. His family pioneered the district."

Bronte slapped a palm to her forehead. "He's a fast mover, all right!"

Gilly demurred. "Well, he's a nice bloke, but I always thought Chika was a bit slow."

"I'm talking about Steven Randolph. Anyone who lost most of their fingers would be a bit slow."

"Chika admitted what he did was very very stupid," Gilly pointed out. "It was years ago anyway. Chika has his boys now, big, strapping fellows."

"Sure. Neither of them over-bright, either. Who'd want to handle man-eating crocodiles for a living?"

"There's an art in it, love," Gilly told her cheerfully. "Anyway Wildwood is only one of Steven's ventures. He and a partner put up a very nice motel with a good restaurant. They use the walls for exhibitions of young artists. A lot of them have migrated here. The North is a glorious place to paint. The motel-restaurant has been a big success. Steven put in a manager as he likes to move on to new projects."

"I expect he thinks Oriole is lovely?"

"Yes, he does."

Bronte smarted. She turned to look back at the emerald blanketed Rex, imagining it as a real dinosaur that had once roamed this land. No wonder Steven loved Oriole. It was a dreamscape! The wonderful fragrances of the fruits and flowers, the exotic character of the place. The North was unique for the luxuriance and diversity of the plant life. She was looking forward to the sunsets. Tropical sunsets were extravagantly beautiful, the sun going down in a great ball of fire, the brief lilac dusk, then star spangled nights with a low hanging copper moon. She turned back to Gilly. "So what's he up to now?" she asked.

"Well I've been dying to tell you all about it," Gilly said, in a deep confidential tone.

Oh, no! Bronte thought. Here it comes! "Does it have anything to do with Oriole?" She crouched down to get a close-up of a beautiful orchid that had taken root in a dead branch.

Gilly prickled slightly at Bronte's tone. "Now, now, lovie. It was my idea."

"What was?" Bronte stood up.

"It's just that Oriole is so *big*, love. And my money is running out. I'd love this old place to come back to life. Steven thinks we can make it happen."

"I bet!" Bronte answered darkly, twisting her head to catch a flight of parrots.

"It will always be yours, love. Or my share of it."

"Share?" Bronte thrust her hair over her shoulder in sudden agitation. "You own Oriole outright, don't you?"

"Of course I do. I'm talking about if Steven and I went into partnership?"

"You're going to farm crocs in the lily pond?"

"This is worth listening to, Bronte." Gilly's black eyes glinted with seriousness. "I'm no fool."

"Of course not, I never meant to imply that," Bronte apologised. Gilly could do what she liked with her own property.

"And Steven is no con man."

"How could either of us rely on that?" Bronte challenged. "Looks and charisma go hand in hand with chicanery." Bronte's concern was written clearly on her face. "Have you checked him out? There's a big backlog in the courts prosecuting charming con men."

"Bronte, dear, I've been fending off con men for years," Gilly scoffed. "Real estate up here is getting *hot!* I haven't been interested before, but mostly for *your* sake I think it's time to cash in on what we've got."

Bronte groaned, terrified Gilly could get herself into financial trouble. And over *her!* "Please don't worry about me, Gilly," she implored.

"Don't be ridiculous! I've been worrying about you for years and years. I can't stop now. Your mother may have married a rich man but I don't think there'll be any mention of *you* in his will. I'm sure Miranda had to sign a pre-nuptial agreement."

Bronte nodded. "She did. Not that she ever told me just what it was."

"You can bet your life she found it humiliating," Gilly said. "I thought you'd be pleased?"

"Gilly, you're free to do anything you want." To calm herself Bronte moved closer to a magnificent stand of ancient ferns found only in the rain forest. Some of them had grown into trees with huge crowns standing twenty feet or more over her head.

"I won't do anything that upsets you." Gilly followed Bronte up.

"We don't really know this man, Gilly," Bronte pointed out as gently as she could when she wanted to yell: *exactly who is he?* "He said he has a law degree. I don't know from where but it should be fairly easy to find out. Another odd thing, he said he knew of Nat's family. He said I wouldn't want to move in with them. He spoke like he actually knew them."

Gilly's expression turned thoughtful. She tucked a snow-white lock back into the loose coils. "Funny, he never said anything to me."

"Yet you told him all about me?" Bronte tried not to sound upset. She knew how proud Gilly was of her.

"Lovie, you can't turn around anywhere in the house without seeing a photo of you. You were on the television until that rotten Saunders struck back. Damned if *I'm* famous compared to you. Steven was interested. He thinks you're very beautiful and a great actress."

Bronte laughed that one to scorn. "I'm not a great actress. Great actresses are born, like my mother. I've got a little talent that's all and I'm photogenic. I'm not a great *anything!*"

Gilly pulled her over and hugged her. "You're too modest, that's your trouble. Give yourself a chance. You won't be twenty-three until the end of December. I thought your parents might have named you Noelle but Miranda had a thing about the Brontë novel *Wuthering Heights.*"

"I know. She's often said it's her favourite book though I've never seen her read anything else. *Vogue, Harpers & Queens, Tatler, Vanity Fair, Architectural Digest,* that's about it."

"She wouldn't have time to *read,*" Gilly said dryly. "That

megalomaniac she married demands all her attention. But getting back to Steven!''

"How long have you actually known him, Gilly?" Bronte asked in a worried voice.

"I dunno." Gilly broke off a dead frond. "It seems like forever. He's been up here quite a while but I didn't run into him until around June. It was after you left anyway. I'd taken a trip into town to do my shopping and Steven was walking out of the mall the same time as me. He asked if he could push my trolley."

"Oh, right!" Bronte said with extreme sarcasm. "That's one way to start up a conversation. He probably knew who you were."

Gilly threw back her head and laughed, a sound that put a dozen brilliantly plumaged lorikeets to flight. "Hell, girl, who am I? Steven sure wasn't after a fling. I mightn't look it but I *am* an old lady. I have to keep reminding myself from time to time. Steven is a gentleman. He unloaded the trolley and put it all in the back of the ute for me. I said I had someone to unload it at the other end, the someone being me, but I didn't let on to him about that."

"So how did he get to visit?" Bronte had a sinking feeling.

Gilly eye-rolled her. "I seized my opportunity next time I saw him in town. I said if he was anywhere near Oriole Plantation sometime he might like to pop in."

Bronte looked at her with eyes like saucers. "Gilly, do you realize how dangerous that was?"

"Don't be ridiculous, girl. You of all people should know I can protect myself. Besides, eyes are the windows of the soul. That young man's eyes are as clear as crystal. If I could go back forty years my ambition might be to marry him," Gilly laughed, heading off towards the lagoon where thick banks of the Green Goddess lily and tall reeds grew around the boggy perimeter.

"I suppose it's possible to become hooked in one's seventies," Bronte mused.

"Shows what you'd know," Gilly said. "Seventy-year-olds are as enthusiastic about sex as seventeen-year-olds. The right man can melt a woman of any age like a marshmallow."

"Good grief!" For some reason Bronte felt herself go hot. She bent in agitation selecting a river pebble and sending it skipping across the smooth sheet of water.

"I'm fooling, sweetheart!" Gilly guffawed. "I'm just trying to get something straight. I trust Steven Randolph like I trust you."

That hurt. "You still haven't told me what he wants you to do?"

Gilly bent, picking her own pebble. She threw it with gusto and it went further than Bronte's. "If you can wait until tomorrow—I've asked Steven to dinner—he can tell you himself. He can explain it all so much better than I can. He knows his way around all the legalities and things like that. He's right on side with the council and he does things properly, anyone in the town will tell you that. Wait until tomorrow night."

Morning. The first rays of the sun filtered through the billowy lemon folds of the mosquito netting that cocooned the huge Balinese bed. A warm golden beam lay across Bronte's dreaming figure, but it was the outpouring of bird song that woke her. She turned her dark head on the pillow. The pillow slips and the sheets had been scented with Gilly's aromatic little sachets. It was a floral-woody smell, that was the closest she could come. Gilly never would reveal her secrets though she'd promised Bronte she'd left her her books of recipes in her will.

It was impossible to sleep with that powerful orchestra tuning up. There were all sorts of voices, violins, violas, cellos, flutes, oboes, trumpets, the occasional horn, even a bassoon. Whistles from those who couldn't properly sing. A loud resounding *choo* from the whip birds. Miaows from the Catbirds. Beautiful singing from the robins.

Lovely! Bronte turned on her back, staring up at the sixteen-foot-high ceiling with its elegant plaster work and mouldings that badly needed restoring. She stretched her arms above her head, luxuriating in the morning and the brilliant performance. It was the first morning in fact she'd woken up not thinking of the terrible fiasco of her abandoned wedding. She fully appreciated now her involvement with Nathan had been engineered by her mother with the full support of her manipulative husband. Both understood the advantages of the match, social and financial. To *them!* Nat never had been interested in her really. Certainly not in her *mind.* He'd been far more interested in her body and the fact she could, when she put her mind to it, look as stunning as Miranda.

For so many years of her life Bronte had looked to her mother for some signs of love, of support, but mothering for Miranda was a closed book. All Miranda's energies in life were directed towards pleasing her horrible husband and maintaining the ravishing looks that were the envy of her socialite friends. Looking back Bronte realized Miranda had been trying to marry her off from probably age eighteen. A girlfriend told her it was because her mother didn't want Bronte around as competition. Gilly had brought her up to scorn vanity so Bronte never thought of herself in that way.

Her own mother jealous? Yet Miranda's critical comments and hard stares whenever Bronte was dressed up to go out could have been interpreted as a kind of jealousy?

It didn't matter any more. She couldn't go home. She couldn't even rent an apartment in Sydney. Like Carl Brandt owned her mother, Miranda thought she owned her daughter. And then there was poor Max, her half brother. She wondered if it would be possible to get Max up to Oriole for the Christmas vacation. He would *love* it! It wasn't as though he had doting parents who required his presence although poor shy Max had knocked himself out for years trying to win a scrap of affection from either one of them.

What a pity no one could choose their parents, Bronte thought. Not that she didn't cling to her love for her dead father. It ran like a river deep inside her. Her father couldn't possibly have meant to end his own life as was rumoured. In doing so he would have left *her,* a defenceless little seven-year-old. Surely he would have thought of that? Ross McAllister, her dad. She just knew God was going to let her see her father again. She'd always been too sick at heart to allow herself to dwell on her mother's relationship with Carl Brandt before their hasty marriage. Who in their right mind would want Carl Brandt for a lover let alone a husband?

Bronte threw back the single sheet, releasing yet another waft of delicious fragrance. Gilly was so clever, she should have been a celebrated *parfumer*—was there such a word?—capturing wonderful fragrances. Or at least a chemist, a botanist, a scientist.

Bronte pulled the mosquito net out from under the mattress then slid her feet to the cool polished floor. She felt like galloping bareback around the plantation but Gilly had been forced to sell Gypsy, her spirited and mischievous chestnut mare, and Diablo, the tall baby gelding, who was no devil at all, but sweet and even tempered. Gilly had always said Bronte and Gypsy were a perfect match, as it had to be if horse and rider were going to enjoy themselves. It was because of Gilly she was such a good rider. This had pleased Nathan. He liked the fact she was so knowledgeable about horses, especially at polo matches which he couldn't really understand. But then she didn't want thoughts of Nathan Saunders to sour her day. He was out of her life. The wonder was he was ever in it. She wouldn't have even crossed his path had she lived a normal life instead of being Carl Brandt's stepdaughter.

Bronte snatched up her silk kimono from the elaborate

carved chest at the end of the bed, then padded across the hallway to the old-fashioned bathroom to take a quick shower. In her childhood big green frogs took up residence in the bath from time to time. Gilly hadn't minded frogs any more than she minded snakes but Bronte hadn't been so keen. She'd wanted the bath to herself. This morning she let the shower run refreshingly cold. It was going to be another hot day but she would soon acclimatize. Back in her room she pulled on some underwear, stepped into a pair of white linen shorts and topped them off with a blue and white striped singlet with a nautical motif. She pulled a leather belt around her waist and tied her hair back in a thick pigtail. The lightest touch of foundation for its high SPF, a slick of lipstick, trainers on her feet.

There, she was ready. All her items of dress were expensive but she'd have been just as happy in the sort of gear she used to wear. She remembered how she'd hated to wear dresses to school. Hated even more the uniforms she'd had to wear at boarding school. Some of the girls—they were all from rich families—had tried to torment her. ''You're such a primitive!'' was an early taunt, until they found out when aroused she had a pretty caustic tongue. Gilly had always insisted she had to be articulate so she could defend herself in a tough world. Later, because she couldn't stop herself wanting to learn, her fellow students discovered she was *clever*. Actually she'd sailed through her years at boarding school the smartest in her class. It was with human relationships she was such a dismal failure.

The morning was spent tidying up the homestead. Despite Gilly's best efforts to keep order—she wasn't at all domesticated—controlled chaos reigned. Gilly had always had a problem throwing anything out. Afterwards they careened around the plantation at breakneck speed in Gilly's faithful old ute. It was a trip that evoked muttered prayers and many a shrieked, ''Slow down!'' from Bronte, not that Gilly took the slightest notice. Gilly considered herself to be an excellent driver. If anyone needed any proof, in over fifty years of driving she had never had an accident. This was something Bronte pointed out had more to do with having the rural roads mostly to herself than good driving practices. Gilly wouldn't have lasted two minutes in the city without being waved down by a disbelieving traffic cop.

Much of the two hundred acres had gone back to an incredibly verdant jungle.

"I can imagine gorillas would be very happy here," Bronte remarked, her feet quite jumpy from all the braking she'd been doing from the passenger seat.

"Are you serious, love?" Gilly swerved madly to ask.

"Of course I'm not!" Bronte laughed. "Listen, what about letting me drive?"

"No way, ducky. I know all the potholes and ditches. You don't."

"You *must* know them. You haven't missed one."

Gilly ignored that. "Once around sixty or seventy hectares were under sugar. A magnificent sight. And the burn offs! Spectacular! Great leaping orange flames against the night sky, the smell of molasses. These days a lot of cane growers have adopted green cane harvesting. That allows the trash to fall to the ground as organic mulch. It reduces soil erosion but in areas of high rainfall like here that method can contribute to water logging the fields. I miss all the drama of the old days."

"Well, the kangaroos and the emus love it," Bronte said, gazing out at a stretch of open savannah where the wild life was exhibiting mild curiosity at their noisy presence but mostly going on their serene way.

"You're not *really* nervous, are you, Bronte?" Gilly had the grace to ask. "I can see your foot moving from time to time."

"Pure reflex." Bronte tossed back her plait.

"You'll come to no harm with me," Gilly said jovially,

demonstrating her skills by ruthlessly sorting out the gears. "This is *our* world, Bronte."

"Our lost world," Bronte smiled. "I'd love to have seen Oriole in its prime."

"Its prime could come again," Gilly's face wore an enigmatic smile. "World sugar prices peaked in the mid-seventies not all that long before you were born. I remember the Duke of Edinburgh—so handsome he was—attending a ceremony in Mackay in 1982 to mark twenty-five years of bulk handling. We led the world in the mechanical cultivation and handling of the crop. Oriole was right at the top in the 1970s, and it was a tropical Shangri-la years back when I was a girl. We lived like royalty in our own kingdom. Then came the war. You know the rest. McAllisters were among the first to enlist. Four of them. My father and his three brothers. Uncle Sholto was the only one to make it home. Such losses tore a great hole in our family."

"They would have," Bronte answered soberly, thinking how tragic it must have been for bereaved families all over the world.

"Uncle Sholto tried to do his best for us but he'd been badly wounded and suffered a lot of pain for the rest of his life. My brother, your grandfather, was so young when he took over. When we lost him in 1979 it was the end for Oriole. Your father had always wanted a different life. He was clever and ambitious, making his mark as an architect. I often think if he'd stayed at home he'd still be alive today."

Bronte's heart lurched. "Oh, Gilly, why do you say that?"

"Sorry, love, maybe I shouldn't be saying it. I don't want to hurt you but I'll never forgive Miranda for what she did to my nephew."

"What did she do?" Bronte asked quietly.

"She destroyed him."

Bronte sucked in her breath. "You truly believe that?"

"No escaping the facts, lovey." Sadly Gilly shook her head. "Miranda tried to pass off young Max as premature but you and I know differently. Not that I believe for a moment Ross threw away his life, he loved you far too much. It was an accident, tortured minds become careless. Your father never meant to leave you.''

"My mother said he loved speed.'' Bronte looked off to the left where the trees of the rain forest met McAllister land. The savannah grasses had been scorched golden but the forest was in deep emerald shade.

Gilly's voice vibrated with long suppressed anger. "She had to say something didn't she? Speed may have been a factor but I'll never believe any other explanation than Ross's mind was elsewhere.''

"I was lucky I had you, Gilly.'' Bronte's voice lightly trembled.

"Darling girl, it was *you* who turned me back into a human. Around here I was becoming known as the witch of the North. I had to shake myself up with a child in the house. I came to love you so much I was devastated when you had to leave me.''

"I hated going away,'' Bronte told her. "I'd been hoping my mother had forgotten about me. Why do you suppose she suddenly remembered she had a daughter?''

"I don't know.'' Gilly yanked on the gear stick. "Maybe she thought you might finally be an asset. You got prettier and prettier every time she saw you.''

"Which was like once a year,'' Bronte's mouth turned down. "I wanted to ask you. Would you mind if Max came to visit in his school holidays?''

Gilly shot her a slightly chastening look. "Of course I wouldn't mind. But I can't see your mother letting him come. Just for spite. She'd hate for him to enjoy himself up here.''

"Maybe she might.'' Hastily Bronte adopted the brace position as Gilly floored the accelerator to tackle another ditch head on.

"Made it!'' she whooped in triumph as they bounced high then plunged deep across. "Why don't you write to the boy?

I don't suppose you can ring him at the school. We've got plenty of room. I suppose we'd better start getting back to the house. What are we going to give Steven for dinner?''

"What do you usually give him?" Bronte asked in a supercilious voice.

"Have you forgotten? I'm a terrible cook. I was hoping you would do the honours."

"Really! You've got me up here to cook for Steven Randolph. In that case there'll be a choice of cured kangaroo," Bronte offered, deadpan, "or fricassee of baby crocodile's tail with stir fried noodles."

"You're joking, aren't you?" Gilly asked, alarmed. Gilly's all time favourite was boiled eggs.

"Don't you worry," said Bronte. "I'll put on a great meal. What time is Action Man arriving?"

"I know you're going to be nice to him?" Gilly asked, mildly nervous. "I said, six-thirty for seven o'clock. Drinks on the verandah before we move in for dinner. Steven's great company and you're going to enjoy yourself, love. That's a promise!"

Bronte looked at her sceptically. "I only know one thing for sure, I'll be keeping a very sharp eye on Steven Randolph at all times."

Bronte had difficulty deciding what to wear. She wasn't going to dress up for the man, Gilly's heartthrob or not. For one thing he might get the wrong idea. On the other hand she couldn't offend Gilly who considered it impolite not to dress up for the rare guest. She'd only brought a couple of dresses with her anyway, trousers being de rigueur in the jungle. She looked at the two pretty summery dresses on the bed. One was a floaty white chiffon printed with big red flowers and swirls of green leaves. The other was a simple slip top with an asymmetrical skirt in imperial purple. Of course she'd bought it because of the colour. It did wonders for her eyes.

Steven Randolph was going to miss out on the pleasure of seeing her in those. She ought to be able to get away with what she called her pyjama outfit—a halter neck top with slinky long pants. The fabric was an understated gunmetal, but in certain lights it looked silver.

"What's *that* you're wearing?" Gilly asked, when she walked into the huge, old-fashioned kitchen. "You look gorgeous!" Gilly rolled expressive black eyes. "You've got just the right figure for trousers. I'll have you know I had a great figure in my day. Great hair and skin, too. Hell, I don't know why I lost my fiancé, I was a lotta woman."

"You still are, Gilly," Bronte smiled. "I love your caftan. Very Marrakech. Your fiancé couldn't have been terribly smart."

"He wasn't," Gilly snorted. "I think he'd planned to take me for every penny I had then found most of it was tied up with the land which I'd never sell. But I was in love with him at the time. He used to sing to me, you know, accompany himself on the guitar."

"Good grief! That's the first I've heard of it," Bronte said, trying to visualize the young Gilly being serenaded by her caddish fiancé.

"Well I have to keep one or two things up my sleeve. Speaking of which, what are we having for dinner?"

"It's a wonder we're having anything," Bronte said. "This kitchen might be as big as a football field but it wouldn't thrill a serious cook. In fact, Gilly, the major appliances would make a serious cook seriously unhappy."

"That's all right, love," Gilly said complacently. "Cooking isn't my passion."

"Whilst I on the other hand undertook an excellent cooking course to prepare myself for being a good wife to Nat." Bronte moved over to the hob. "Controlling the heat on this is downright impossible. There's no such thing as a simmer, no moderate heat, it's all a raging boil. But I haven't let you down. We're having something nice but simple. The whole barramundi is in the oven as we speak. It should take around forty-five minutes. I've stuffed it with prawn meat, egg, cream, sherry, mushrooms, and surrounded it with cubed vegetables. It's going to be delectable. The seafood certainly came in handy. Obviously your Steven knew he was coming to dinner. There's a little dill sauce to finish. I couldn't begin to tackle an elaborate dessert, but as the oven's on, we're having baked paw paw in coconut milk with toasted shredded coconut on top. There'll be mango ice-cream, too, and I've already roasted a bowl of nuts, mostly our own macadamias to nibble on with drinks. Tomato and mozzarella for an appetizer with anchovies draped on top. I think he'll go home a happy man.''

''Any complaints and we'll push him out the door,'' Gilly joked, obviously in high spirits. She placed a lovely pottery bowl full of avocados on the sideboard then made for the door, the dozen or more silver bracelets on her arm setting up a jingle. ''When you do get really serious about someone, Bronte, you'll make a wonderful wife.''

''That's not my idea, Gilly,'' Bronte called after her.

Not *my idea at all!*

Steven Randolph arrived bearing gifts. Wine, Belgian chocolates, and something in a cardboard box tied with a brown-gold striped ribbon.

''Thought it might come in handy,'' he said, kissing Gilly on both cheeks and slanting Bronte a smile. Not a serious smile. A quirky one, that uptilted the corners of his shapely mouth. ''I'll take these into the kitchen, shall I?''

''You know you didn't have to do that.'' Gilly beamed on him.

''A pleasure, Gilly. You look great!''

Next he'll be saying the two of us look like sisters, Bronte thought waspishly, leading the way to the kitchen. He certainly had Gilly hooked. Was he the second man in Gilly's life trying to take her for every penny she had? Over my dead body, Bronte privately fumed.

"Don't you want to see what it is," Steven Randolph asked her, as Bronte set the cardboard box down on the long narrow pine sideboard. He was busy putting the wine away in the fridge. Gilly, excited and happy, had drifted out onto the candlelit verandah, no doubt pushing them together.

Bronte smarted. "Give me a minute, can't you?"

"I'm sorry. How *are* you?" He allowed his eyes to move over her. She was so beautiful with those enormous black fringed blue-violet eyes but as spiky as a cactus. A cactus in an outfit like liquefied silver. It looked almost like lingerie. It took a huge effort not to reach out and caress it...*her*. But he'd never met a girl who so clearly signalled *keep your distance!*

"I'm fine, thank you." Bronte fought her way through the ribbon which securely tied the box. "Gosh, this looks good!" The comment flew out of its own accord.

"Gilly loves chocolate."

"I *know* that!" She flashed him an irritated glance which he met with a quirky one of his own. He looked really cool. She had to admit that. He was wearing a very smart black shirt with a cream stripe teamed with beige trousers. He really did have a great body. That aggravated her.

You better be darned careful, Bronte, she told herself. *This man is dynamite!*

"Why are you so desperate to put me in my place?" he was asking in an entirely reasonable voice.

"Put you in your place?" Bronte raised supercilious brows. "I thought I was only talking to you. Where did you get this scrumptious looking confection?"

"It's a fruit and chocolate brandy cake, by the way." He turned away to find a plate.

"Thank you," she said pointedly, accepting it. He knew where everything was kept.

"Be careful getting it out."

She knew he was trying to get a rise out of her. For a moment she considered dropping his offering. Instead she calmly and efficiently removed the large cake from the box. It was covered with a glistening chocolate icing and decorated with silver balls.

"I made it myself, actually," he said, getting a finger to a tiny dollop of chocolate icing left inside the box and putting it slowly into his mouth.

She looked away from him, determined to keep her reactions on ice. "You did not!"

He laughed. "I had to say something to get you down off your high horse. The truth is, Bronte, I know a very nice lady I can turn to when I want something special."

It wasn't the question to ask, but she did. "Do you sleep with her?"

"What?" He rolled his clear green eyes upwards. "Bronte, you shock me. This lady makes cakes for heaps of people."

"That's all right then. The thing is we don't know very much about you, do we, Steven Randolph."

His green eyes smiled. "Why don't you ask is that my real name?"

"Is it?"

He smiled. A sensual mouth above a determined jaw. "Bronte, you're about as sensitive as an armed tank," he said.

"That's okay." She shrugged off the jibe. "This is confidential. Would you mind telling me, if you're not married *now*, have you been married or engaged?"

He picked a lemon leaf out of a bowl and began to flick it backwards and forwards under his nose. "Don't you think you're being a teeny-weeny bit *pushy*, Bronte?"

"No I don't," she answered bluntly. "I'm simply taking the precaution of finding out a few more things about you."

Mockery glinted in his eyes. "I've never had much difficulty finding a girlfriend. Does that make you happy?"

"Honesty makes me happy and I hope I'm getting it.

While we're on the subject, don't waste your time trying to chat *me* up.''

He laughed aloud. "Fine, no problem. Truly, Bronte, I wouldn't dare. Anyway, you'd have to lighten up a lot to get my attention."

"I've been getting your attention from the moment you walked in," Bronte returned tartly.

It was something he couldn't hide. "Well you *are* very easy on the eye," he admitted, carelessly turning his mahogany, sun-streaked head away. "What's that baking in the oven? It smells marvellous."

"Compliments are of no use to me. As for what's baking, as if you didn't know, it's the whole barramundi you put in the fridge. You know the one Gilly ordered when she knew you were coming to dinner and which you faithfully delivered. She didn't bother to tell *me* until today."

"It must have been a nice surprise." There was a mocking glint in his eyes.

"I haven't made my mind up yet," Bronte said.

CHAPTER THREE

IF BRONTE served up a delicious dinner, Steven Randolph served up the charm, though it came as no real surprise he was good company. Bronte had set the table in the main dining room which was rarely used, but it housed a remarkable collection of maritime paintings and a handsome antique mahogany dining room suite which looked wonderful with a polish. Like Gilly who had an endless flow of conversation, their guest had many an amusing story to tell. In fact when Bronte finally relaxed under the benign influence of a couple of glasses of a beautifully balanced Riesling with the aroma of apples, flowers and citrus, she found herself laughing a lot. Even liking him to her shame. Or liking him up to a point. They hadn't as yet come to the main item on the agenda—what sweeping plans he and Gilly had in mind for Oriole.

Otherwise they had a lot in common. Favourite authors, films, art, love of travel. Like Bronte's late father, Steven Randolph told them he loved architecture—naturally he *loved* Oriole's homestead—he'd once wanted to be an architect, he confessed, but his father had dissuaded him telling him unless he hit the very top there wasn't much money in it.

"Why did you listen if that's what you wanted?" Gilly took another big gulp of the lovely wine.

"I was seventeen at the time." He shrugged. "I guess it was all to do with toeing the line. My father wanted me to study law."

"Your father's a lawyer?" Bronte asked, feeling free to question.

Steven gently swirled the wine in his glass, staring down

at the golden-green liquid. "Yes." For once his answer was clipped.

"What's he like?" Bronte asked, trying to read the expression in those clear green eyes which also managed to be unfathomable.

"The sort of man you don't question and remain on side with," Steven answered dryly.

Bronte understood all about that. "You're saying you're not on side?"

"Bronte, you're not going to delve into my private life?"

"Indeed I am! Gilly's told me none of this."

"For the very good reason I didn't know," Gilly blinked. "Steven hasn't actually spoken about his family."

Bronte turned her attention from her great-aunt back to their guest. "So you're not close, you and your father?"

He leaned back in his splendidly carved high backed mahogany chair. "Bronte, I have to tell you, my father has cast me adrift."

"Really?" Bronte and Gilly exclaimed together, equally amazed. He didn't look, sound or act in the least like a man whose father would cast him adrift.

"As in you had to leave home?" Bronte asked, feeling a twinge of empathy.

"I didn't live at home, but yes, I left. Physically and spiritually. I have an older brother who is everything I was supposed to be, so that's okay. I won't be missed."

He sounded more matter-of-fact than bitter. "Sisters?" Bronte looked at him. He was perfectly at ease with women.

"No. Just two sons. Some minds allow themselves to be moulded. Others fight it. I let myself be talked out of architecture for a career, but I wasn't going to be talked into beavering away with corporate tax."

"What firm?" Bronte sat bolt upright for the answer.

He looked amused. "Since I'm no longer part of it, Bronte, there's no need to say. It's not relevant to my life, and I'm surprised I'm telling you about it at all."

"Well, I can always find out the *hard* way," Bronte pointed out. "But surely talk about one's career and family is the most natural thing in the world?"

"Is it?" he responded, a faint taunt in his expression. "Let's start with your stepfather, Carl Brandt?"

"Struth!" Gilly picked up a silver dessert spoon and lightly struck her glass. "Let's leave Brandt out of this. Callous brute!"

Bronte stared into Steven Randolph's handsome face. "Carl Brandt is not my family. He's not my father. He's my mother's husband."

"A fine distinction."

She looked across the gleaming table at him. Gilly sat at the head. Bronte and their guest faced each other across a silver bowl of white orchids. "Why do I have the idea you know a lot more about me than you're saying?" She was still grappling with the notion.

He didn't answer immediately, studying her expressive face. He liked how she had done her hair, drawing it straight back from her face, high on the crown, the silky blue-black masses cascading down her back. "What I know about you, Bronte, I've learned from Gilly. She loves you. You're her favourite topic of conversation."

"That's true," Gilly confirmed fondly. "Bronte is all I've got in this world. She's very precious to me."

"Actually they should have named me after you," Bronte patted her great-aunt's hand.

"That would have been a punishment, love," Gilly laughed. "You're definitely not a Gilly. So, Steven, go on. You were telling us you left?"

He nodded. "I inherited money from my mother. It wasn't long after that I made my decision to get out."

Bronte felt her heart contract. "So you lost your mother?" she asked in the gentlest voice he had yet heard from her.

"Yes. She died a week before my twentieth birthday."

Bronte waited for a few moments, staring at his down bent

head. His right hand that had been lying relaxed on the table had stiffened into a fist. "I'm so sorry," she said.

"Yes, dear," Gilly seconded, placing a sympathetic hand over his.

"You sound *angry* underneath?" Bronte found herself saying.

His handsome head lifted and he smiled crookedly. "So much for keeping any secrets from you, Bronte."

"What about coffee?" Gilly intervened, steering the conversation away from the painful. "And a slice of that lovely chocolate cake you brought, Steven. I still have a little room left, though that was a delightful meal, Bronte."

"Indeed it was. Congratulations," Steven added suavely.

Bronte gave him a little barbed smile. "I did so want to please you."

"Well you've succeeded," he drawled.

"What about the coffee?" Gilly reminded them, looking from one to the other. "Quick! On your feet."

"I'll get it." Bronte went to rise. Immediately he was there to hold back her chair.

"I'll help."

"Ever the gentleman, Steven," Gilly said with an approving smile. "Pile it all on the trolley," she suggested, well pleased with how the evening had gone thus far. "Later we'll have to get on with discussing our plans for Oriole, Steven. Bronte is anxious to hear them. One day everything I have will be hers."

The coffee was excellent, and the cake every bit as good as it looked. Bronte managed a sliver for politeness unlike Gilly and their guest who got stuck into it, there was no other word for it. Empty cups, saucers and plates went back onto the trolley which Steven Randolph returned to the kitchen. Con men took pleasure in their work, Bronte reminded herself. At least they had learned something more about him. His own father had disowned him! It was quite an admission when he seemed determined on remaining a man of mystery. This didn't suit Bronte at all. If one invested trust in someone and one's *major asset* like the family home, it was essential to know all there was to know. The normally cautious Gilly wasn't paying sufficient attention. It was Bronte's job to look out for her. Gilly had been too busy soaking up the charm.

The draperies in the drawing room were looking the worse for wear. The once lovely fabric had been faded by the strong sunlight, the silk trim unravelling. In fact everything needed restoring, the soft furnishings, the woodwork; the large, high ceilinged room had been outfitted with handsome golden panelling that needed attention, as did the parquet floor strewn with still glowing oriental rugs. There was some very fine furniture in the house, mostly oriental pieces, cabinets, altar tables, elegant chairs as well as Chinese porcelains and glazed stoneware, and objects from India and South East Asia—like the Burmese Buddhas, reclining, sitting, standing. There was even a Chinese opium bed somewhere—European and Australian art, not pretty pictures, seriously *good,* but it had been so long neglected or shoved around that the house had lost nearly all of its old grandeur.

It was sad. It was a great house. A wonderful house with a welcoming feel. There was only one hitch. It would take a fortune to do it up and Gilly didn't have one. Neither did Bronte. She had knocked back a fortune when she had knocked back Nat Saunders.

Randolph returned. He looked so handsome, so vibrantly masculine Bronte considered he should be viewed through smoked glass. "Well, I'm waiting!" she said meaningfully.

"You look great in that chair." He held her with his green gaze. He'd known she was wary of him from the moment he set eyes on her, so oddly sweet with a tart centre, rather like a delicious chocolate. The light from the big crystal chandelier, put a sheen on her; her skin, her hair, the satiny clothing she wore with such glamour.

"Isn't it marvellous!' Gilly enthused, turning her attention to the elaborately carved chair in question. "One of a pair. Goodness knows where the other one is. It should be in here. Indian, of course. Just look at that carving. One of the ancestors, Sandy McAllister, General Alexander McAllister that is, brought them back with a whole swag of stuff. Maybe *he's* got it." Gilly spoke as though General "Sandy" popped in and out of the house on a daily basis.

Steven settled himself in an upholstered armchair, facing both women. "I know we all agree this is a wonderful house that should be brought back to life," he said persuasively. "It could be done in this way, as a business venture. Oriole is obviously far too big for one person to manage, and Gilly has told me of her difficulties. I see it as a secluded retreat for a select number of guests who value their privacy and the natural beauty of their surroundings.

"The mix of the rain forest and the proximity of the sea and the Great Barrier Reef is irresistible to overseas tourists. We know that for a fact. The plantation doesn't want for space, and there could be some beautiful trails established for those who enjoy horse riding. The stables would be brought back of course. The food and the service would have to be first class; buffet breakfasts, lunches, presented al fresco perhaps? The climate is perfect for most of the year. We might have to shut up shop in the Wet and we'd need to put in a swimming pool right away. In time there could be guest houses, but right off, there would have to be accommodation for staff. Not many staff but indoor and outdoor people. Top of the list, a chef. The gardens could be brought back to looking wonderful. This sort of hidden retreat is in demand. The atmosphere of a private home in a guest house."

Bronte waited a full half-minute before she spoke. "You can't see any risk factors in any of this?" she asked grimly, knowing she had to keep her cool "Perhaps you could tell me how we could possibly finance a project of this sort. Gilly doesn't have a fortune hidden away, you know."

"That's okay," he said in his smooth sexy voice. "The banks will listen."

"Sure of that, are you? I say they'd baulk at it."

"Why don't you let me handle that part of it, Bronte," he replied smoothly. "We can come up with a viable proposition."

"Isn't the crocodile farm glamorous enough?" Bronte asked tartly.

Gilly sniggered.

Even Steven laughed. "Look, I'm the *brains* of that outfit. I'm not the brawn."

"What a shame! You look the part. Besides they say crocodiles become quite affectionate in time."

"Bronte, you just made that up," Gilly said, her hair frothing around like a white fog.

"I thought I'd say it anyway." Bronte glanced at Steven Randolph, catching him watching her with so much interest her outfit might have been made out of tulle. Her colour heightened. "Even if you had $100 million at your disposal, you wouldn't want all this upheaval, would you, Gilly?" she pleaded. "At your time of life? Can you imagine what it would be like living here with all the restoration and building work going on? The noise! The chaos! Workmen traipsing all over the place."

"I'll be able to cope," Gilly said, a glow of animation in her cheeks. "After all, I've been hiding out most of my life. Grieving for a fool of a man who never loved me. I want a bit of excitement instead."

"For a short time you might!" Bronte countered. "You can bet your life it'll be more trauma than excitement. You've been used to solitude. I thought you loved it."

"Maybe I'm fed-up," Gilly said. "I'm tired of being known as nutty old Gilly."

"You're *not!*" Steven Randolph assured her. "You have quite a reputation in the healing business."

"Hardly a complaint in darn near fifty years," Gilly

crowed, pulling at a magnificent emerald ring she whipped out on rare occasions and wore on her right hand. Not her engagement ring. The ring had belonged to her mother. "Wouldn't you love to see Oriole the way it used to be, Bronte?" she asked almost prayerfully. "When I was younger it used to be my fantasy, but of course I didn't have the money. You can see for yourself, love, this wonderful old house is going to wrack and ruin."

"It is not," Bronte stared about her, sincerely hoping the ceiling wouldn't cave in. "It just needs a darn good clean-up and some mild restoration. Anyway…" She turned her attention back to their guest.

"Steven," he prompted, amusement in his eyes.

Bronte pressed her lips together. "Anyway, *Steven,* you seem to be confident of handling the finance side of it, but I'm not. Haven't you got enough eggs in your basket not to take on anything else?"

"I'm a phenomenon," he explained, a faint taunt in his eyes.

"Does that mean basket case?" she asked acidly.

His eyes sparkled. "On the contrary, so far my ambitious plans have come off. It's not a massive project after all. We're not going to start big. We're going to proceed in stages."

"Oh, this is ridiculous!" Bronte cried, agitated despite her efforts to keep calm. "Gilly doesn't realize what something like this could entail."

"I think I do, love," Gilly said sounding very unthreatened. "Anyway I'm game enough to try."

There was worry in Bronte's beautiful violet eyes. "Gilly, have you thought you could *lose* everything?"

"Steven and I don't intend to lose," Gilly said. "We're going to be partners. I put up Oriole and Steven finds the money to make it all happen. Steven, this week if you've got time, you should show Bronte your motel," she suggested.

"I've got an even better idea, you could take her to dinner in the restaurant. The poor child needs reassuring."

"Well, of course I do!" Bronte cried. "I'm looking out for you, Gilly. I love you. You know I'm not going to allow you to get into any financial or emotional mess. Oriole has been in the family for well over one hundred years. That's a long time in this part of the world. This is frontier country. Think what General Sandy would say if you lost it."

"He's had his say already," Gilly informed her.

"He's a wraith. He can't talk," Bronte pointed out briskly.

"The fact is I receive messages," Gilly said. "They tell me this is going to work out, Bronte. Besides, it's all for you. You don't want to go back to your old life, do you? You weren't happy. You hate your stepfather. Your mother does nothing but try to railroad you. Look at your engagement! Not your idea at all."

"Do we have to talk about that?" Bronte wailed. "I believed I loved Nat."

"Rubbish! You're just saying that so you won't feel bad."

Bronte stared from her great-aunt to Steven Randolph, sitting back so confident and relaxed. "You're both serious about this?"

"It's not going to be nearly as harrowing as you suppose," he said, his attitude reassuring but surprisingly *firm*. "Gilly's right. I'm busy tomorrow afternoon, but you should see the motel. It might allay some of your fears. We could even run both projects in conjunction. Motel in town near the beach. Oriole with its wonderful rain forest setting and your own private mini-volcano. The restored homestead and the tropical gardens would be a marvellous setting for a wedding come to think of it."

"*No* weddings," Bronte said, and shot him a withering look.

"Okay," he said mildly, "but in no time at all you'll find it hard to remember your own nonevent. If you're agreeable, we could have dinner at the restaurant. It's so popular even

I have to book. As a very good cook yourself you can tell me what you think. Shall I make that for the three of us?'' He gave Gilly a positively beautiful smile. No wonder he'd had no trouble cementing the friendship, Bronte fumed. He was pulling out all the stops!

''No!'' Gilly laughed, miraculously looking ten years younger. ''Take Bronte. I want you two young people to get to know one another.''

Knowing Gilly the way she did immediately raised a very big question in Bronte's mind. Was Gilly trying her hand at matchmaking?

''Well?'' Steven Randolph looked straight at Bronte, raising his well defined brows. Women probably went down like nine pins when he looked at them like that.

Not her! She'd had a rough time with men. Bronte mused a moment. ''All right then,'' she grudgingly acquiesced. ''It will give me an opportunity to discuss this matter more thoroughly.''

Gilly broke in. ''We can hardly expect you to drive back to town, Steven.''

''No bother!''

''You do realise you're over the limit?'' Bronte asked with polite sarcasm.

He shook his mahogany head. ''Not at all. As you've been counting, Bronte, you'll know I've had the same as you. Two glasses. You're the one who could be over. Women can drink less as we know. I've found if I stick to two, no problem.''

''That makes me feel better,'' Bronte said.

''It doesn't make me feel better,'' Gilly interrupted. ''We've got tons of room. I really don't think it's necessary for you to make the long drive, Steven. Indulge an old lady. Spend the night. You can take off whenever you like in the morning. Okay?''

''You win, Gilly.'' He smiled.

"In that case, let's open another bottle of wine. It was beautiful. I was really enjoying it. I don't sleep very well these days. It might help."

Bronte woke from a sound dreamless sleep. At least not a dream she could remember. It was early. Very early, yet she felt wonderfully refreshed. Steven Randolph hadn't left. He had stayed the night she suspected to please Gilly. She had to hand it to him. He gave every appearance of really liking Gilly and enjoying her company. She had brought Nat to Oriole once to meet Gilly. It had been a disaster. Nat had seen Gilly as a nut case. Gilly had seen Nat as a "pompous idiot!" Of course with Steven Randolph it could all be an act. She'd witnessed her awful stepfather charm people, worldly people one would think would know better. But then at the heart of society was gross insincerity.

Once awake she couldn't remain in bed. She decided she'd make herself a light breakfast and go for a walk before it got too hot. That way she'd probably miss Steven Randolph's departure, and Gilly could do the honours waving him off.

Dressed in frayed shorts that had actually cost a handful and an azure bikini top Bronte opened her bedroom door very quietly and listened for the slightest sound of activity. Nothing. No one stirred. Gilly unused to much alcohol would probably sleep in. Steven Randolph being a man might be looking for a cooked breakfast around eight. It was rare to meet the man who didn't want to be waited on. Her mother, famous for her selfishness, played the role of devoted wife to the hilt. She would even lay out her dear husband's clothes for the day and for his social engagements. What was even more surprising Brandt accepted her judgment in silk ties. But then Miranda had exquisite taste and the perfect eye for detail.

Bronte moved through the old house with its marvellous old ghosts, padding in bare feet over the oriental rugs and the polished floors. It was so silent she could almost hear her heart beat. Pools of pearly dawn light fell through the unshuttered French doors. She was still listening intently but she was safe. No one was about. No one being Steven Randolph.

She almost fell into his arms.

"Hi there!" he said. "You're up early."

He'd touched her. He was touching her, his hands on her bare shoulders. It was a tremendous shock. She knew she should move away fast, say something about grabbing a cup of coffee and going for a walk, but his touch was so *electric* she felt riveted to the spot.

"You startled me," she said, gaining control again. "I didn't think anyone was about."

He dropped his hands. "You mean you *hoped* I wasn't about."

He turned on his high voltage smile. He was wearing the same clothes he had worn last night, but he'd left more than half of his shirt unbuttoned. She couldn't unglue her eyes. She saw a muscular chest, deep bronze skin, a light pelt of body hair. It churned her up and she didn't like that. This man aroused her big time. It was an involuntary thing. She had to master it.

"It's a beautiful morning," he was saying. "Cooler than yesterday. Maybe you'd like to join me for a walk?"

She replied in her most off-putting voice, an excellent imitation of her mother, dreadful snob. "Don't you have to get back to town?"

"Well, no, not this very minute."

He seemed more amused by her responses than offended. "Have you had something to eat?" She looked past him accusingly to the kitchen from which he'd emerged to startle her.

"Actually I was going to make coffee. I thought I heard someone moving about so I came to look. Join me?"

Bronte gave up. "Sure," she said.

He let his eyes dwell on her. Something about her made him near sick with longing for he didn't know what. It was a feeling without parallel. Everything she wore looked *elegant,* even a sleek little bikini top that showed off her delicate, beautifully shaped breasts, and a pair of artfully tattered shorts. She had lovely limbs, this beautiful prickly vulnerable girl.

He made her sit down at the kitchen table while he ground the coffee beans releasing their wonderful fragrance, set up the percolator then cut slices of bread for toast. "Feel like a mango or a slice of paw paw while you're waiting?" he asked.

"You really know your way around here, don't you?" Bronte lifted brooding eyes to him.

"Why don't you trust me, Bronte?" he asked. "What is it about me that raises all your hackles?"

A couple of heartbeats went missing. "I don't want to see Gilly exploited," she offered. That was true certainly but there were other disturbing reasons. All he'd been was nice to her yet he made her feel increasingly wary as if she was about to fall into his trap.

"You can hardly believe I'd do that?" Deftly he sliced up two large mangoes he'd taken from the fridge, placed the sections in a bowl and lightly spritzed the succulent fruit with fresh lime juice.

"Truth is, I don't trust *anyone,*" she admitted with real sadness. "Outside Gilly that is."

"Why is that?" He found plates and forks, set hers before her.

Bronte meditated briefly. "I learned early it doesn't pay to trust people," she said. "Much less give your heart away."

"But you haven't given your heart away, have you?" His green gaze locked on hers. "You *couldn't* have loved Nat Saunders?"

Bronte shrugged. "At this point in my life I only *love* Gilly. Love, pure and sweet. I try to love my mother, and I have loads of affection for my half brother. His name is Max, a kind gentle boy. Too gentle for his own good. Very clever, too, not that he gets a word of praise from his parents. For all his brains he won't be strong enough to enter his father's world.''

''Why would he *want* to?'' Steven asked with what sounded like contempt. ''At present he's dependent on his father but if he's got faith in himself he can break away at some point in the future.''

''If he's not broken before that.'' Bronte shook her head. ''I want to get him up here for the school vacation. He's only fifteen.''

''Yes.''

There, he'd done it again! ''What do you mean, yes?'' Bronte asked, sounding utterly exasperated.

''Well, he'd have to be some years younger than you,'' he pointed out reasonably.

''Damn it all, do you *know* my stepfather?'' Bronte demanded to know.

He gave an exaggerated sigh. ''Bronte just about everyone has heard of your stepfather, Carl Brandt, the corporate predator.''

That was Bronte's view but she didn't want to hear it from him. ''Tell me this then, why hasn't he gone to jail or are all big businessmen white collar criminals?''

''Ask around,'' he said laconically. ''Eat your mango.''

''Oh for goodness' sake. Why are you so keen on humouring me?'' Bronte stuck her fork into half a mango cheek.

''I think you're going through a bad patch, that's why.'' He finished off his share of mango and set down the plate. ''One slice of toast or two? Or are you working at keeping that model figure?''

''Two slices, thank you,'' she said tartly. ''Keeping my figure is no problem.''

''I suppose so at twenty-two. You might have to cut back when you're forty.''

"I don't like you, Steven Randolph," Bronte said, feeling an inexplicable hot ache at the pit of her stomach.

"I'm not exactly sure I like you." His dark warm tones deepened with amusement. "But then we don't have to be friends. Look on me as a business partner."

"It's not *my* money," Bronte said.

"That's okay. You'll perk up when you see the motel and restaurant," he promised, pouring the hot, black aromatic coffee. "I'll pick you up around seven. Make sure you're here."

He was actually making fun of her! "What is that supposed to mean?" Her cheeks flushed with anger.

"Nothing really. You're just such a complicated girl, Bronte. You may well take it into your head to lock yourself in your room and refuse to come out."

She shook back her ponytail. "I'll never live down abandoning my wedding to Nat Saunders."

"Don't feel bad," he said, taking butter and spread out of the fridge. "It's probably the best thing you've ever done."

CHAPTER FOUR

THE motel, called The Bamboo Lodge, turned out to be a very pleasant surprise. It was quite different to what Bronte had expected, the usual sort of concrete box-like structure with parking bays at the front. The Bamboo Lodge was a series of timber guest bungalows, set beautifully and unobtrusively into tropical gardens. The bungalows surrounded the restaurant, a two-storey building with a subtle feel of a Thai pavilion.

The grounds were floodlit so Bronte could see the landscaping had been carried out with great flair using the huge range of tropical palms, ferns, flowering shrubs and plants the area was famous for. The entry to the restaurant was very attractive, with magnificent cycads massed along the front façade. Two life-size bronze sculptures of the native birds, the brolgas, stood on the emerald-green patch of lawn. Only natural materials appeared to have been used, timber and stone with expansive areas of glass. Although the complex appeared spacious she could see it wasn't *big,* but certain to attract the tourists who looked for quality and beautiful, natural surroundings.

"What do you think?" He'd let her take it all in before asking the question.

"I'm impressed." Bronte was busy looking around her. "It's not what I expected at all. A far cry from the bland, conventional motel."

"That's not what we wanted," he said, his hand still at her elbow as they negotiated the short wide flight of stone steps. "The idea of the bungalows surrounding the restaurant appealed to me. My partner liked the idea too so the whole project evolved from that."

"The feel is Asian?" His hand on her bare skin was breaking up her concentration. "I've visited Bangkok several times with my mother. Pukhet, Hong Kong and Singapore."

"We do live in this part of the world. Personally I love Asian art, architecture, cuisine. You've got a lot of Asian furniture and artefacts at Oriole so one of your ancestors obviously loved them as well. Those big baluster vases Gilly uses to shove banana leaves into are very valuable. K'ang His, probably early eighteenth century. You might like to move them to a safer spot."

"Have you upended them to look at the markings?" She couldn't resist asking.

"No need to," he said. "I've got quite a good eye." He paused at the top of the steps to look down at her. "You'll be meeting my partner."

"He's not dining with us, is he?" To her relief Bronte kept her stupid, involuntary disappointment out of her voice.

"No, of course not. I would have told you before this. My partner is a woman. Christine Ching Yee. She runs the restaurant."

"Oh!" Bronte sensed Christine Ching Yee was an exceptional person.

"You'll like her," he said. "She's very cultured, speaks several languages, smart as a tack at business with a marvellous knowledge of Thai and Chinese food. She doesn't do the actual cooking, but she oversees everything, the menus, the flowers, the changing décor. Not a thing escapes her."

"So I'd better be appreciative?" Bronte said.

"I'm sure you will be," he promised. "Christine was born in Singapore but she spent most of her childhood in Thailand with her mother's family. She married a journalist who covered stories in the region. Tragically he was killed, so Christine's alone now."

Bronte thought she detected real *feelings* for his partner in his voice. "There's a lot of heartbreak in life."

"So much one doesn't like to speak about one's own. Shall we go in?"

The Thai mood was confirmed from the moment they stepped inside. The restaurant was called The Vanda Room after the beautiful blue orchid native to Thailand. Sprays of them were included in an eye dazzling arrangement of flowers that stood in a big blue glazed bowl on a carved stand in the foyer: lilies, liliums, anthuriums, a wide variety of beautiful orchids, the blue vandas, Queensland dendrobiums, flights of phalaenopsis, the butterfly orchids, the showy phaius, the giant among Australian terrestrial orchids mixed with fragrant sprays of foxtail orchids in various shades of ivory, magenta and pink. Bronte drew closer to admire them. The flowers had been faultlessly arranged. She saw some species of orchids she didn't know but she thought they looked like members of the pineapple family.

When she turned back a small slender woman was walking—no, *floating*—towards them, arms bent at the elbows, graceful hands outstretched. A pose that might have looked theatrical on anyone else.

It had to be Christine. Bronte didn't know what she'd been expecting, even what age group, but Christine Ching Yee was stunning. Her very beautiful skin glowed like a golden pearl.

"St-e-ven!" She had the very slightest, charming lisp.

Towering over her he bent and kissed her on both flawless cheeks. Her gleaming ebony hair was parted in the middle and drawn back behind her ears. She wore an ankle-length Thai silk skirt in Chinese Imperial yellow, a little matching top, very chic, cut away at the shoulders and exposing her golden midriff, high heeled yellow sandals.

She looked terrific. Absolutely nothing like Bronte had been expecting. What a night for surprises!

Steven Randolph introduced them. Bronte received a handshake, a little bow and a calm smile. "Welcome, Bronte. I'm so very pleased to meet you. Next time you come you must bring your aunt, Miss McAllister. Steven has told me so much about her, I'm most anxious to meet her. I hear she is a natural healer with a wonderful knowledge of rain forest plants.''

''It's been her lifetime interest,'' Bronte explained. ''May I say that floral arrangement is breathtaking. It *is* yours?''

Christine nodded, taking the compliment in her stride. ''I adore arranging the flowers. It brings me peace and relaxation. Now, I'll show you to your table. We have one or two special things on the menu. I want you to so enjoy your evening.''

''I'm sure I shall,'' Bronte murmured, feeling for the first time in her life tall and awkward beside this tiny graceful creature. It was impossible to tell what age she was. She could have been anything between twenty-five and thirty-five. Even a perfectly preserved forty. There was a world of experience in the eyes.

''Your partner is very beautiful,'' Bronte said sincerely, when they were seated at their window table overlooking the garden and Christine had moved off to greet arriving guests.

''Thai women are exquisite,'' he said, with male appreciation in his eyes.

''How did you meet?'' She asked the irresistible question.

He looked directly at her. ''In Thailand. Christine was a guest at the same function I attended for a Thai princess. We got to talking. She told me quite a bit about herself. How she'd lost her husband. I've visited Thailand many times since boyhood so the conversation sort of flowed. Naturally we got around to talking Thai food which was of huge interest in her mother's family. She said then she'd love to open a restaurant one day. We kept in touch. When this block of land became available I had the idea for a motel with a first class restaurant. It was then I contacted Christine. By the greatest good fortune she was interested.''

''She must have money?'' said Bronte, looking back at him thoughtfully. ''Money is essential for business partners.''

"Yes, she had money," he answered calmly. "But then I had my inheritance."

"Well, congratulations," Bronte added warmly, not wishing to be churlish. "I love all this." She looked around the large room with pleasure. The restaurant was filled but it wasn't noisy. It was humming quietly. She could hear a mix of accents: Japanese, Chinese, American, German, English, Australian. The young waiters and waitresses wore the same uniform. Black pants, cute little white jackets with gold buttons that fit snugly at the waist. The tables were set with crisp yellow cloths and napkins, almost the exact colour of Christine's outfit. Bronte wondered if the colour changed from night to night.

The teak and bamboo chairs were elegant and comfortably shaped. The small centrepiece on their table—Bronte had noticed the adjoining tables were different—consisted of four different leaves, of different shapes and lengths, each enhancing the other, and a single flower. A perfect purple iris. It was deceptively simple and amazingly attractive. On the long wall to their right, hung a very striking oriental screen of multiple panels depicting wonderful calligraphy on a gold leaf ground. On the opposite wall a glass case framed in ebony displayed a collection of exquisite fans, silk, ivory, mounted on lacquered sticks, some with an appliqué of ivory and unusually gorgeous colours.

Steven followed her fascinated gaze. "You're admiring the fans?"

"How beautiful they are!" Under their influence, she gave him a lovely, relaxed smile. "I'd love a closer look some time. There must be how many? Fifteen, sixteen?"

"Sixteen," he said. "I've counted. The collection belonged to Christine's Chinese grandmother. She inherited them along with the screen on the wall. She has a collection of really fine jade and painted snuff bottles. I'm sure she'll be happy to show them to you."

"It makes me feel I'm of no interest at all," Bronte murmured lightly. "So much history. So much background. It's wonderful Christine has allowed guests in the restaurant to admire her treasures. Doesn't she worry a visitor might take a fancy to something? Quite obviously they're valuable possessions."

"There's an excellent security system. Giving pleasure makes Christine happy." He eyed the collection again. "The fan is a purely Chinese invention."

"Is it?" Bronte showed her surprise. "I didn't know that. If I thought about it at all I would have said it came from Europe. France or Spain?"

"You're not alone in thinking that. Even scholars have made mistakes. The earliest known example was found in Hunan province dating back to the second century BC. Even then the design was so sophisticated it suggested a much earlier history."

He was pretty cultured himself, Bronte thought. And clever. Surely this enterprise was proof of that? But she was by no means won over. "Easy to understand how fans came to be made," she mused. "We can't be without them in our heat. Older women continue to carry personal fans. Gilly has stacks of them at the house. Nothing like Christine's. Gilly's are mostly functional, though she does have a few ivory fans now I come to think of it."

"The homestead is a treasure box," he said, lowering his handsome head so she could see he had a perfectly straight nose.

A treasure box he could hardly wait to get into?

"Christine's collection would have been part of the elaborate language of court etiquette," he went on. "They were more art objects than functional. China first started exporting fans to the West in the seventeenth century. Christine can tell you far more than I can. She's the expert. I can see you with one of those fans in hand, designed for a man's entrapment."

Some expression in his eyes sent a frisson shooting

through her. "Your friend Christine would handle one better." She was certain of that.

"I don't know. Very few men would be proof against *your* charms. Which one would you choose? Something to go with that dress." He let his eyes flow slowly over her. She was wearing a slip of a dress in the most beautiful shade of deep violet. She looked simultaneously extraordinarily sexy and strangely innocent. It was an odd mix, one he hadn't encountered before. Something about her made his heart contract as if he'd known her when she was a child. A sad little girl dismissed by her own mother.

"The one with the gorgeous blue on the leaf," Bronte was saying, knowing she was going pink. Things were turning out very differently to what she intended. With his distinctly sensuous gaze on her she felt like she was being caught up in a strong current that was hurtling her to him. There was no chance of swimming against it.

"Macao blue," he said. "My choice for you, too. You won't be able to see from here but the vignettes are little scenes from court life. Christine will be pleased you like her collection. Her collections are her children."

Bronte touched a painted pink fingernail to a petal of the iris. "She's a beautiful woman. Surely one day she'll remarry and have children of her own. Where does she live? May I ask?"

"Not with *me,* Bronte McAllister," he said, sounding amused.

"I didn't mean that." Her blush deepened.

"Yes, you did. Let's get it out into the open. Christine is my business partner and my friend. I'm very fond of her. She's brave and tough and clever."

"Goodness, I wish someone would say that about me," Bronte sighed.

"Well, it was brave leaving Nat Saunders," he pronounced.

"Absolutely right! And horribly difficult."

"Well, then you're brave," he congratulated her in deep, honeyed tones. "I *can't* think you're tough."

"I don't like tough people very much," she said, lifting her chin. "*You're* tough."

"So we're not going to hit it off?" He mocked her with lazy charm.

"You didn't mention clever. It may be a revelation to you to know I have a higher than average IQ."

"Of course you have." He smiled at her in a way that made her both nervous and incredibly conscious of being a woman. "What are you going to drink, champagne?"

His smiles were flustering her. Probably he was just playing around or this was a complex ploy. She didn't much believe that just good friends routine about Christine. Bronte knew she hadn't received the radiant smile he had. "Well…" She forced herself to relax again. Play it cool. "One glass would be lovely."

"Great!" He signalled the waiter.

There was no way she could call herself a good cook after sampling The Vanda Room's menu. She hadn't had better food even at the Bangkok Oriental, one of the great hotels of the world.

"This is marvellous!" she said in a surge of fairness and appreciation, forking daintily into an entrée of Thai style crab salad with green mango. "Who exactly would the chef be, if Christine isn't? I think I'm going to go to the trouble of personally thanking him for such divine food. Plus it's given me lots of ideas. I have to find a job, you know."

"You're not going back to your acting. And you were so *good!*"

"Are you making fun of me?" she asked sharply.

"No, no, not at all." He waved a chopstick which he had handled very deftly to pick up little morsels of spicy crisp fish with very finely sliced lime rind. "No way would I have missed one of your shows."

"You *are* making fun of me," she said. "Never mind. I spent a lot of my adolescence being put down and fighting my way up. I was very touched by all the letters I received after Nat's father canned me. If Nat's mother had had her way she'd have lynched me."

"No way that marriage would have worked," he said, accomplishing wonderful things with those chopsticks.

"So you've said before," she frowned helplessly. "Look at me."

It was a mistake of course. He gave her his full attention, his green eyes brushing her face, her mouth, her shoulders, the mauve shadowed cleft between her breasts. It was overwhelming. Even on her guard she had never experienced an arousal of this magnitude. It sent an actual stabbing pain to her nether regions.

"Well?" he questioned. "You're an utterly beautiful woman and immensely appealing despite the prickles."

"And you're playing around." Her violet eyes were eloquent with scorn. "For a *reason*."

"Of course I am," he said. "Finish your entrée. I'm ready for my mains, sautéed beef with black pepper sauce. The way they arrange the dish is something to see—the green baby vegetables and always some other vegetable cut into an exquisite shape."

Bronte stuck with the seafood, lobster served with a crispy gnocchi salad. Not only did the food taste delicious the artistry of the presentation contributed much to the enjoyment. Once Christine paused briefly to ask if everything was to their satisfaction, her jet black eyes lightly flicking over Bronte's face and dress, perhaps calculating the price?

"I'm seriously impressed," said Bronte.

"I'm so glad to hear that." Christine touched Steven Randolph's jacketed shoulder lightly. "Could I have a private word with you before you go? It won't take a minute. You don't mind, Bronte?"

"Of course not." Bronte was thinking the other woman

couldn't care less if she did. Christine Ching Yee was absolutely gorgeous, Bronte thought. A porcelain doll. An astute businesswoman. Brave and tough. A linguist. Yet Bronte hadn't taken an instant liking to Christine any more than she felt Christine was charmed by her. It occurred to Bronte the reason was Steven Randolph. He sat there looking as sexy as hell in an elegantly slouchy linen suit that went wonderfully well with the mustard coloured T-shirt he wore underneath.

Pretty cool! Bronte wasn't feeling all that good about how he was pushing her buttons. And so easily. She took a dim view of her own weakness.

Bronte waited in the foyer while he had the promised word with his partner, Christine. She found herself loath to watch him giving the other woman his attention which was decidedly unsettling. She couldn't even begin to ponder the cause. The two of them stood together, the one so supremely vibrantly masculine, the other the epitome of delicate femininity. Bronte focused once again on the dazzling flower arrangement. She would have liked to have pulled out one of those blue vandas and kept it but diners at the restaurant were trusted not to pull the arrangements apart. She turned back at the very moment they were saying their goodbyes. The way he kissed his partner on both cheeks though it appeared a sophisticated little ritual unsettled her afresh. What business of hers was it anyway? Her own sexual attraction to him had to be set aside. She'd shut right down on that kind of thing. Entanglements only led to trouble.

Afterwards they strolled around the curving pathways in the grounds so Bronte could get a better idea of the complex. In the great soaring dome of the sky, so soft, so velvety, the stars blazed brilliantly. The incomparable scent of the Torch Ginger was borne to them on the cooling night breeze, gardenia, oleander, perfumed plants all around them. An unwilling excitement was pouring into Bronte's body which was awkward to say the least. She'd intended to keep her distance. She'd have loved to slam the lid on it but it was proving near impossible. His tall, lean body was so close to hers, occasionally brushing when a frond from a golden cane got in the way. It put her into a highly defensive state. His hand cupped her elbow when the path ahead led into shadowy pockets leaving her half trembling.

There were several sticky minutes when she felt like taking to her heels like a panicked adolescent. After the fiasco with Nat she had thought herself immune to romantic dalliances. She wanted something different. Peace and quiet. Now this near stranger was making her lose all her composure. In fact he seemed to have a genius for it.

When he murmured it was about time to take her home she nodded vigorous agreement. "I don't like the idea of Gilly being on her own," she said in her most responsible voice.

"She's always on her own."

He laughed which made her intensely angry.

When some nocturnal creature made a sudden leap across her feet, she actually recoiled, slamming back into his shoulder. "Oh!" she gasped. "Things that go bump in the night."

"It's okay." His tone was indulgent, almost tender. "It's only a tiny little frog. You're not frightened of frogs are you?"

"How could I be frightened of frogs when I've actually eaten their legs," she said indignantly, thinking how she had done it for a dare at a Paris restaurant. One anyway. She'd hated it. "For your information, I'm not frightened of frogs, Steven Randolph if that's your real name. I near jumped into your arms because I think you're incredibly sexy. Is that more like what you were expecting?"

"What are you on about now?" he laughed.

"If you *dare* kiss me," she found herself issuing the warning, convinced he was about to do so. There was no smile now. His eyes glittered. The level of awareness soared.

"Listen, Bronte," he said very softly. "Beneath the words,

I'm getting a different signal. I've been getting it loud and clear all night.'' He drew her to him, an action so smooth he must have spent a great deal of time perfecting it.

"I'm sorry. It's just one of your fantasies.'' She sounded cool enough, but her whole body was flushed with heat.

"Let's check that out.'' He threw down the challenge, manoeuvring her into a pocket of velvety dark. An enchanted arbour. Fronds of palm trees hung above them, gardenias blossomed radiantly in the lush greenery. It was a long, long time, if ever, since Bronte had experienced such arousal yet he was making it seem the most natural thing in the world.

"Who hurt you, little girl?''

Oh, his *magnetism!* The sexual presence. She couldn't credit it or the way his hands were so gently, erotically, cradling her face. She scarcely knew what to answer, so disconcerted by everything about him. She knew now what it meant to get *lost.* "I'm fine. I'm over it,'' she managed to say huskily. "I don't know what we're doing here like this, Steven. What this little interlude is all about. I don't understand you.''

"Hell, Bronte. I don't understand myself.'' He gave a little groan. "If it were a full moon, we could say it was moon madness.''

"Others might describe it as calculated seduction.'' Whatever it was, she'd already grasped the fact he was going to have his way. And she wasn't going to put up a fight. Temptation was too strong.

The moment held such intensity her heart did a somersault as he lowered his head. She breathed in his male scent before his mouth actually touched hers. It was strangely intoxicating, enhancing all other sensations. She must have made a sound but he silenced her, his mouth covering hers so gently yet so voluptuously she was transported instantly out of this world. He wrapped her tightly into his arms, cocooning her like she meant everything to him, the sole object of his affections, the fulfilment of his dreams.

Such was his power it could have generated enough electricity to light the entire town, she thought dazedly.

Who for instance had ever kissed her like this? So beautiful, so natural, radiating heat and desire? Whose tongue had ever flipped across her lips, shaping her mouth as if it found it fabulous? More urgently, how could this lovemaking continue and remain unconsummated?

The groan in his voice snapped her out of it. "Bronte… Bronte…what are we going to do about this?"

Do? She had a disturbing vision of herself as his willing slave. Bronte took long moments to disengage from him, desperate now to sober up. "Don't get your hopes up," she warned. "There's nothing between you and me but business. Not even that. Gilly will be your partner. And only if things work out."

"So you don't want an affair?"

"No." She nodded. Just like a robot.

"What a pity! You mightn't be tough, Bronte, but you're a great kisser." He lifted a hand and gently caressed her cheek.

"For the record this is the only time you're ever going to get to kiss me."

"Really?" His voice mocked. "Well, it was worth it. But don't panic."

"I'm not panicking," she said sharply. "I'm continuing along the path before somebody comes after us."

"Who could that *somebody* possibly be? What a touchy person you are." He caught her up, sliding his arm companionably through hers as though they were the best of friends. "It's a miracle I've warmed to you so quickly."

There was silence inside the car. The atmosphere was so *charged* it was incandescent. Bronte was so strung out she was spurred to speech. "With so many projects going," she began in a businesslike tone, "The Bamboo Lodge appears to be a success though I don't know anything about the occupancy level of the motel—''

''High, it's generally full,'' he interrupted her briefly.

''I see. However, the point I'm trying to make, yet again, is haven't you got too many things on the agenda?''

''Success can't stand still, Bronte.'' He glanced at her. ''There's another aspect we need to factor in. Oriole is falling down around Gilly's ears. She's an amazing woman but she's ignored maintenance on the homestead. It's obvious it's been neglected for many many years. The grounds before the clean-up had almost reverted to jungle. I fully expected to see monkeys swinging through the trees.''

Bronte's reply was tart. ''You know perfectly well we don't have monkeys.''

''No, but you had a million brushtail possums that had the great good sense to make their escape to the rain forest. Snakes galore. Try stepping on one and see how you go. The fact is Oriole is a superb property that could be turned into a beautiful and successful retreat. Not big. Not anything that would involve a huge amount of work but well able to draw the discerning guest. As I've said a limited number through the Dry. Very few would choose to holiday in the Wet although the country on the verge of the Wet, like now, is glorious. I always think it takes the coming of the Wet to bring the bush to flower.''

''I know that a darn sight better than you do.'' She knew she was being childish but she couldn't seem to help it.

''Well, sure you do.'' He shrugged. ''I know all about your years with Gilly.''

''Then you know my mother didn't want me,'' she said very tartly, though she had the most vulnerable expression on her face.

How he sensed her pain! He wanted to stop the car, hug her as tightly as he could. Kiss her lovely face, wipe away the tears. She'd borne up remarkably well for all she'd endured. "You think of yourself as an abandoned child?" he asked quietly.

"Certainly not." She was still on the defensive. "I was a *deprived* child who wanted desperately to be loved."

"Why not?" His tone was sombre. "It's every child's right to be loved, though we all know rights get trampled on."

"And a child must accept everything that's done to them." She spoke more bitterly than she intended. For years she had trained herself to remain separate from her pain.

"Sounds like we're talking damage here, Bronte. Damaged parents rear damaged children. Destructive parents have children who ultimately go on to repeat learned behaviour. Not all, but many. Having a child is a sacred trust. Not everyone has the ability to cope with that."

"My mother certainly didn't," she sighed. "Gilly was my *real* mother. I won't allow *anyone* to hurt her."

"What kind of great-niece would you be if you did?" he asked. "I hate to say this, but you won't be helping Gilly by getting in the way of progress."

"Progress being your becoming her partner? You're just such a humanitarian!"

"Look, don't get upset."

"Oh for goodness' sake I *am* upset." Her voice betrayed her rising anger. "Lately I'm having difficulty holding on to just who I am. But I know this. I'm here to give support to Gilly not you. I don't even know you. I certainly don't know your whole story."

"I'm *not* a hustler, Bronte. I'm a respected businessman. I want to help Gilly. She thinks—I think—she's up to the challenge. She said herself she's taken a back seat in life. Oriole has been her bolt hole. A hiding place. A great pity! There was no need for Gilly to lock herself away."

"She was desperately unhappy."

"She could have worked through it with help."

"She didn't have help. She had no one. I think she must

have had a nervous breakdown, poor Gilly. She's so clever she should have been someone. Something. A scientist.''

"I agree. But she turned her back on the future to live in the past."

Her throat grew tight. What he was saying was true. Gilly could have married and had a family. She had the ideal place to raise children. Oriole. Gilly had been meant for better things. "It's too late to talk about that now."

"It's not too late to talk about bringing a sense of happiness and achievement into her life. I know Gilly's age but she's no ordinary woman. I'm convinced she'd cherish this challenge. She wants to see Oriole brought back to life. She refuses point-blank to sell it. Oriole is *your* inheritance. It could be a life interest. At the very least an excellent investment."

"And you're equally convinced you can raise the money? We don't want any more partners, you know."

"We certainly don't. I've got used to doing things my way."

"Really? And Gilly and I are supposed to trust you to handle the job alone?" She glanced at his strong profile visible in the lights from the dash.

"Christine did. She's nobody's fool."

"Did I mention the word, *fool?* Christine is a beautiful, clever, cultured woman. I'm talking about *you.* You surely don't think Gilly and I are going to sit around twiddling our thumbs while you run the show?"

"Of course not!" He sounded exasperated. "Especially when it comes to refurbishing the homestead. I'm expecting a lot of input."

"Darn right!" She nodded vigorously.

"You know, Bronte, you've been angry with me since you first laid eyes on me."

"Granted."

"What's the reasoning there? The answer can't be simple. I'm certain if you had me checked out thoroughly and I passed every test with flying colours you'd still be a mass of prickles.''

''It's not generally how I am.'' His accusation brought her face-to-face with her odd antagonism. Primarily it was *sexual* as though she feared she wouldn't be able to hold true to herself if she gave in to him. She knew better than most what it was like living with a controlling male. She simply didn't feel she could take the strain of coming under the influence of another one. Not that Steven Randolph bore the slightest resemblance to her stepfather. In fact he was nothing like him. So why the smouldering hostility? And why the passion?

''So we're not dealing with something rational?'' Steven summed up.

''Maybe you represent something I don't like,'' she suggested. ''That's the best I can come up with.''

''Something or somebody? There's a deep reservoir of hurt and anger in you.''

''Hey.'' She turned her head to him. ''Did someone tell you you had a talent for psychoanalysis?''

''I'm only telling you what I think. A lot of what we do can be tracked to early loss. Children with a sad past hardly have a chance to bloom.''

''You sound like you know a lot about it?''

''Maybe I do. I encountered a lot of difficulties growing up. I know I endured a lot of things that were pretty hard to handle. I had to live my own life. Not fail, succeed. Make a mark in the ledger. I haven't allowed myself the luxury of excuses.''

She regarded him closely. ''You sound *driven*.''

''I am. I know I am. If we're going to work together, Bronte, I want us to be friends.''

''Friends?'' She didn't hide the discordant note. ''How can that be? I can't fit another friend into my life.''

''You could *use* one,'' he said crisply, effectively shutting her up.

CHAPTER FIVE

BRONTE sat at the dining room table continuing her inventory of the homestead's contents. There was a vast amount of stuff in the house, much of it stored away and still to be gone through. Art works of all kinds: paintings, statues, marble busts—why busts? they always stopped short at the *neck*—objets d'art of all kinds and cultures, antique furniture, valuable rugs oriental and Persian, a huge amount of china and crystal, at least seven very beautiful dinner sets, all intact, some looking like they'd never been used, silverware, a collection of Meissen amorini, exquisite little cupids all winged, armed with bows and arrows to pierce the heart she'd never laid eyes on in her life. She'd found them tucked away in boxes in a seldom opened walnut cabinet—for the very reason one of the doors had been stuck for years—along with a collection of small Limoges boxes and one hundred and one Staffordshire animals, mostly dogs.

Whatever was in the house of value she was determined to list it. The bric-a-brac didn't count. For all Gilly's talents housekeeping wasn't one of them. She preferred to be tramping the outdoors exposed to the elements. Gilly would be at home in wildest Africa photographing rhino wallowing in a mud bath, a pride of lions taking pleasure in the evening meal, a lofty giraffe turning a benign eye on the camera. Being outdoors for Gilly was the key to happiness.

It was she who found Bronte beavering away in the dining room, examining and giving an item number to a deep dish with a broad flat rim and a decoration in relief—it had to be a fish—in the centre.

"Careful with that, love. It's Sung," Gilly casually announced, plonking herself in a chair.

"You're kind of calm about it, aren't you?" Bronte set the dish down carefully. "That means it has to be over a thousand years old?"

"Like me," Gilly said with ease. "That piece was in the General's collection. Celadon. A beautiful glaze! There's stuff all over the place."

"I know. You can't move for it."

"That's why you're such a good girl doing all this cleaning up."

"I'm enjoying myself," Bronte said and she was. "You know, Gilly, your friend Steven called the homestead a treasure box."

"He's said that to me as well." Gilly smiled fondly, showing her trust in the man. "Of course I don't press him on the subject of his family, but I reckon they have to be in some kind of privileged position. He's obviously well educated and well bred. He's widely travelled for such a young man and he's managed to fit in a law degree as well. He knows a lot about South East Asia, art and architecture. He even designed The Bamboo Lodge."

"Now why wouldn't he have told me that?" Bronte exclaimed, feeling piqued. "I should have guessed. It's a wonder you haven't met Christine by now?"

"Darling girl I rarely get into town. Only now and again. You know what I'm like. I like to stay on the farm."

"She's very beautiful, very exotic. An excellent businesswoman."

Gilly gave a broad smile. "So you've told me a dozen times already. She must have impressed you?"

"She'd impress anyone. She looks very worldly, very experienced, if you know what I mean. Has he ever said how old she is?"

"Good heavens no. Surely you could tell. I thought you told me she was *young?*"

"I'm still grappling with that one," Bronte confessed. "She could be twenty-one or a hundred and one."

Gilly laughed almost gleefully. "So tell me how does she do it? Don't be silly, child. You sound like you're a wee bit jealous?"

Bronte turned her attention back to her lists. "Now you're being silly. What have you got in your pocket? You keep patting it."

"My old pal Jimmy Wang dropped off our post. I've been saving it." Gilly drew a couple of envelopes from the flap in her khaki cargo pants. "One is from your darling mother, probably asking can she come and stay with us. I'd recognise that flowing hand anywhere." Gilly passed the letter over.

"I wonder what she wants." Bronte held on to the letter as if she were totally opposed to opening it. "Maybe Max has spoken to her about coming for Christmas?"

Gilly gave a none too ladylike snort. "If he has, you can bet your life she says no. Of course she'd miss the boy terribly I don't think."

"It's not as though she and Brandt don't like to go somewhere to escape the heat. They both adore Paris."

"And your mother can buy lots more clothes she doesn't need. I read somewhere she's never seen in the same thing twice. Is that possible?"

"Very possible with Mother," Bronte said, feeling her heart sink as her eyes fell on her mother's elegant penmanship.

The tone was glacial. Miranda didn't send greetings or admissions of missing her daughter. She didn't ask after Gilly or enquire if Bronte was feeling better let alone if she was enjoying herself. It was sterner stuff.

"How dare you go behind my back inviting Max up to that horrible house that's full of snakes!"

The same jungle horror that had sheltered her for five formative years of her childhood.

Max would *not* be accompanying them to London and Paris this year—Max had never been known to accompany his parents anywhere—Max would be staying with a good friend from school. Magnus Potter's boy. Should that mean something? Potter must be a millionaire. The only kind of person Miranda considered worth knowing. She went on to repeat how deeply Bronte had disappointed her and Carl who had done everything in his power to secure a brilliant match for her. Nathan was said to be suffering badly. Threatened suicide was the rumour, but he had settled for soldiering on.

"You broke his heart, Bronte. You might just as well have stabbed him."

Stabbing was never what Bronte had in mind. The rest of the letter continued in the same vein. Bronte had to swallow several times. The upshot: she was not forgiven. Would never be forgiven. Max wasn't allowed to join them in that frightful spirit ridden mansion.

"From the look on your face Max isn't coming?" Gilly's sympathetic smile masked her anger. Miranda was no different now to what she had ever been.

Bronte nodded, her hurt and disappointment evident. "I'd read it out to you but you wouldn't want to know. She never had the slightest difficulty putting me on a plane to visit you."

"For which I am thankful! Only because it suited her own plans to have you out of the way."

"She understood marriage to Carl Brandt had a price. They weren't to be distracted by children."

"He must have loved it when Miranda told him she was pregnant with Max."

"Maybe Miranda saw it as forcing his hand. Anyway Max has suffered and so, too, has my mother. I bet there are a lot of things she bears in silence."

Gilly reached out and patted her hand. "You always were a compassionate little thing."

"She *is* the only mother I've got. The funny thing is, she truly believes this house is haunted. It freaks her out."

"Give me a break," Gilly snorted. "Not haunted, love. *Blessed.* The human spirit can never be destroyed. Our ancestors are more home bound than most. As for your mother! I did see her once tearing down the stairs shrieking her head off.''

"That was a snake. It got into the house," Bronte informed her. "A tatty little garden snake. She told me once she was afraid to sleep here. Every time she woke up some-one was bending over her."

"It was probably the General roaming around," Gilly said, complacently, picking up one of Bronte's lists and trying to read it. "He's always looking for something to do. What are all those lists about?"

"I told you. I'm cataloguing everything of value, Gilly, under the various sections—paintings, furniture, screens, rugs, etc. I'm going to label them. That is give them all an item number. If anything goes missing I'm going to know about it."

"Excellent, excellent!" Gilly laughed.

Bronte studied the dear familiar face of this elderly woman whose love had sustained her. "You know, Gilly, you think you're broke, but you're not. You're actually a rich woman, but short on cash. You could raise it auctioning off some of your possessions. The maritime paintings in this room alone would fetch a lot of money."

"What's a lot of money?" Gilly asked, not sounding terribly impressed.

Bronte leaned back in her chair, staring at the oil paintings on the wall. "Who knows! I don't know which is worse. To have too much money or not have enough? As far as I can see with too much money families fall apart. Not enough they fight but stick together. It's love that makes the world go round. Why then is love so hard to get? And when you get it how do you hold on to it? Some people seem to enjoy giving others as hard a time as they possibly can. Take poor Max and me. Our mother has made an art form out of giving us hell.''

"She did marry the devil," Gilly pointed out. "Maybe he

introduced her to his world? Probably knew she'd fit right in. What happened to the other wives? Numbers one and two?''

Bronte's blue-violet eyes widened. ''How should I know? No one will talk about it. It's not as though he's a nice bloke. People are scared stiff of exchanging any gossip about him. He could have them eliminated for all I know. But getting back to the paintings. I'd say every last one of them would be worth at least thirty thousand dollars. Probably a heck of a lot more. I'm no expert but I've been to many art showings. You'd collapse at the prices. The Australian landscapes are very valuable. So, too, are the seascapes.''

''Why would I want to sell them, dear girl?'' Gilly asked softly. ''They're old friends. I grew up with them in this house. They've always been there. What would I do without my ships sailing around the room? What they're worth doesn't matter. They're priceless because they're my *family*. You're my family. They go to you.''

''I would treasure them, too, Gilly. But selling off a few treasures would enable you to live out your life peacefully and in comfort.''

Gilly stamped her booted foot. ''The problem is, lovey, I want a bit of excitement before I die. Why only the other week Steven promised he'd take me up in a helicopter. We could go over to one of the islands he said. The Coral Sea and the Barrier Reef islands look glorious from the air. The colorations in the water go from aquamarine through turquoise to cobalt. It's years and years since I visited the jade islands. I know you're worrying this is all going to be too much for me, Bronte. You're a good, loving girl, you were as a little lost child, but it's what I truly want. My inheritance has been neglected far too long. It's been decaying like me. We're going to be brought back to life.''

Bronte knew she couldn't fight this. ''Then we need a good lawyer to protect your interests,'' she said.

''We've got Steven.'' Gilly's black eyes lit up.

"You're too trusting, Gilly. So he's shown me what appears to be a thriving motel-restaurant. What do we *really* know about him?"

"I listen to my gut feelings, girl. Since he arrived up here he's established an excellent reputation. Not only that he's the nicest young man I've ever known. When he came out here and saw the place going back to the jungle he moved straight away to clean it up."

"No doubt he saw an opening," Bronte suggested caustically.

"Now, now, he isn't like that at all, Bronte. Living under your stepfather's roof has made you suspicious. Something I fully understand, but not all men are bastards, love. Mark my words, Steven Randolph will treat us right."

"Lord help him if he doesn't," Bronte muttered darkly.

A few days later Steven Randolph rang to say he would be driving out to the plantation that afternoon if that was okay? That was a little nicety Bronte all but treated with one of Gilly's unladylike snorts. He would be bringing a man he wanted them to meet, a widely experienced garden designer who had agreed to visit the site and give some advice.

"What sort of advice?" Bronte asked, her mind seizing on the worst possible scenario. Massive land clearing. "And how much does he charge?"

"Don't get the cockatoo feathers up." Steven's taunt travelled down the phone. "Believe it or not, Bronte, he's doing it for a favour."

"That's wonderful you have so many friends."

"I'd be dropping in anyway," he told her, his voice dropping a couple of seductive tones. "I want to check you're as beautiful as the last time I saw you."

"Then I'd better go and get ready now," she said sweetly and hung up.

Gilly's reaction was expected. "How lovely! I miss Steven

when I don't see him. Have we got something for afternoon tea? I just love your chocolate brownies.''

"You want me to bake for Steven Randolph?" Bronte asked, constantly left astonished by Gilly's affection for a darn near *stranger!*

"Not if you don't want to, love, but you know what they say. The way to a man's heart is through his stomach."

Bronte didn't feel capable of answering for a moment. "You're not trying your hand at matchmaking, are you, Gilly?"

Gilly rose from her planter's chair, digging her fingers into her thick chignon as though she expected to find a little lizard had taken refuge there. "You know I never thought of such a thing in my life. It will come as a surprise to no one that I've been antimarriage in the past. Now I see it was not for the best of reasons. I'd like to see you nicely settled before I go."

"Before you go *where?*" Bronte tore down the front steps in pursuit of her great-aunt.

"To the angels, love." Gilly swirled about to inform her. "If you ask me Steven's taken a real shine to you." She laughed with delight.

"Well I haven't taken a real shine to him," Bronte flared up like a fire cracker, knowing she was caught midway between the truth and a lie.

"That's because that Nat fella left a bad taste in your mouth. Pompous—"

"Gilly!" Bronte shook a warning finger, a severe look on her face. When it came to haranguing Bronte's ex-fiancé Gilly took flight with swear words.

"Steven is a good person. I'm proud to call him my friend," Gilly concluded, before turning back to shove a huge Chinese coolie hat on her head. "I tell you what else I like. Steven would like it, too. That lovely lemon sponge. Sweet things charge my batteries."

"You'd live on them if I let you," Bronte said wryly,

blessing the fact abundant fruit and nuts hung off the plantation's trees, otherwise Gilly, living on her own, would be seriously undernourished. She had all but given up cooking, but she still enjoyed a good meal when it was presented to her.

"That's what comes of getting old," Gilly called, stomping away in the direction of the new chook house.

The day was blazing with heat and fuggy with humidity. The coming of the Wet saturated the air with rich fragrances, as though the volcanic red soil beneath them was coming to the boil. The rear gardens smelt like mangoes in heavy syrup as the great trees dropped their bursting overload of ripe fruit to the ground. An army would have to work overtime trying to eat it all. There were the creamy bananas, too, the paw paws and the papaya, the guavas and loquats, even the rows of strawberries Gilly was intensely proud of but Bronte secretly thought much too big and meaty. Often looking at the overflowing abundance Bronte wished she could box it all up and send it to people in need. All that bounty going to waste! How lucky they were who lived in the tropics. The citrus groves, covered in flowers and bees, promised a bumper crop. Bronte had visited many places but Oriole was not only her sanctuary, it was the place she loved most in the world.

Steven Randolph and the garden designer arrived at three o'clock, right on afternoon tea time. Bronte watched the two of them get out of the 4WD and walk towards the house. Both men wore bush gear and Cuban heeled boots. Steven Randolph's handsome mahogany head was bare, his companion wore a brown akubra crammed well down over his head. Both men were very tall, especially with the boots, the older man much heavier set, especially in the chest, but still in good shape. Somehow he looked vaguely familiar.

In the relative cool of the verandah Bronte waited to greet

them. A welcome afternoon breeze had sprung up lifting the
blossoms off all the luxuriant shrubs and spilling them over
the emerald-green grass. Gilly was inside the house hunting
up photographs of the homestead from the early days.
"They're somewhere in my belongings!" she cried hope-
fully.

"Hi, there, Bronte!" Steven called, sketching a salute.

"Hello. You're right on time." Bronte was intent on the
older man walking beside him. As they came closer she realized she *did* know Steven's companion. It had to be Leo
Marsdon, who had landscaped her stepfather's Blue
Mountain retreat while she was still at school. Now this was
a coup! Why was she being so suspicious of Steven Randolph
when he could get Leo Marsdon on site? Marsdon had an
international reputation. He'd worked on large estates all over
the world. The United Kingdom, his native Australia, France,
Italy, Austria, Greece, Sri Lanka. Bronte's mother collected
all his beautifully illustrated books on garden design. They
decorated coffee tables in Brandt's three houses, city, beach
and mountain, handy to show off to visitors especially the
edition that featured photographs of their splendid mountain
retreat.

"But I know you, don't I!" Leo Marsdon exclaimed, re-
moving his hat as he came up the steps. "All grown up but
I'd know you anywhere. Those morning glory eyes! It's
Bronte, isn't it? Carl Brandt's daughter?"

"Stepdaughter, Mr. Marsdon." Bronte corrected, moving
forwards and extending her hand with a smile. "I recognised
you as well. I'm amazed to see you here. Steven said he was
bringing a garden designer but I never dreamed it would be
you. This is an honour. Surely you're much in demand?"

Marsdon, a fine-looking man in his late fifties, smiled.
"I'm glad to say things go as well as ever, but Steven here
asked a favour and I'm happy to oblige. I've only been home
about six weeks actually. I finished work on a sporting estate
in Argentina, now I'm advising on a waterfront site a little

further down the coast. The way Steven described the plantation and the extensive grounds caught my imagination.''

''Lovely!'' Bronte said. ''My great-aunt will be here in a moment. She's hunting up old photographs to show you. We were hoping you'd have time for a cup of tea?''

''Leo never says no to a cup of tea,'' Steven told her with an attractive twitch of his mouth. ''Afterwards we'll drive around—that's the quickest way to cover the ground. Leo needs to know the nature of the site and the native vegetation.''

''Of which you have a veritable Garden of Eden of diversity!'' Leo Marsdon observed with considerable interest. ''Breath-taking part of the world, the tropics. This is a wonderful old house,'' he turned his head. ''A decided atmosphere, too. It seems to talk to you.''

''An attraction Leo can't resist,'' Steven Randolph said with an amused expression on his face. ''According to Gilly it's because all the McAllister ancestors won't leave.''

''Oh goody! I'm so glad I was invited,'' Marsdon chuckled. ''I feel I can do a lot with this.''

''That's what we're counting on, Leo,'' said Steven.

It was obvious from their interaction they knew one another *pretty* well, Bronte thought, keen to extract some information about Steven Randolph on the side. It was probably only her imagination but she had the impression Steven Randolph had been momentarily thrown to discover she and Marsdon had met before but with his usual cool efficiency he'd covered it well.

''Please come in and take a look around,'' Bronte invited. ''I've been spending my time trying to catalogue the contents.''

''A *huge* job!'' Steven remarked dryly, looking down at her. She wore a glowing fresh flower in her long blue-black hair. It was so alluring he almost bent to inhale its fragrance. He had a sudden mental image of another woman who'd worn flowers in her hair. His beloved mother. As always when thinking of his dead mother a very deep ache started up inside him. This girl, Bronte, her lovely mouth tinged with coral, was wearing a turquoise top held up by narrow straps with a turquoise and white sarong tied artfully on one hip as a skirt. It was an outfit that made her look as cool, as delicate and exotic as a rain forest orchid. He wanted to pull her into his arms. Hold her very close. He wanted quite urgently to kiss her…keep on going… He already knew she was wonderfully responsive for all her tart little tongue. Instead he had to defend himself. "Ah, here's Gilly!" He dragged his eyes away from her, glancing over her head to the hallway, which resounded with brisk, clacking footsteps.

Gilly resplendent in a cream safari suit and brown leather sandals, hurried out onto the verandah. "Oh my, Leo Marsdon," she exclaimed, beside herself with delight. "I'm ready to faint with shock."

"Your fame precedes you, Leo," Steven Randolph said, much surprised. He introduced them with his usual ease and charm.

"I saw a program about you, Mr. Marsdon, a year or so back," Gilly explained. "I never forget a face. Plus the fact I remembered Bronte's stepfather commissioned you to landscape their place in the Blue Mountains. Fancy Steven knowing you! It's our great good fortune." Gilly smiled all round. "I've been rummaging through an old trunk and found heaps of early photographs of Oriole. The homestead and the plantation. You might care to see them, you and Steven. Bronte and I went through them all when she was a little girl but I know she'd like to look again. She's all McAllister."

"And here I was thinking she was Carl Brandt's daughter," Leo Marsdon said. "He certainly allowed me to believe that."

Gilly let out a bark. "Much easier for him I suppose. And Bronte *is* beautiful enough to put on display. But she's my late nephew's child. Ross was killed in a car crash when Bronte was seven. It was terribly sad.''

"Yes, it must have been.'' Marsdon looked kindly into both women's faces, recognising their closeness.

"Do come into the house,'' Gilly invited, leading the way. "A cup of tea is always refreshing in the heat. You must have a slice of Bronte's lemon sponge. She's not only beautiful, she's enormously talented.''

"Ever think of making a career as a chef?'' Steven Randolph's handsome mouth was near Bronte's ear. If she were a bird it would have ruffled all her feathers. As it was, tremulous little ripples of sensation ran down her spine. Maybe he was targeting her with his sexuality and charm? Why did she stand there and take it? Why was she struggling so hard with an attraction that went far beyond anything she had ever experienced before? Maybe as a McAllister she'd have to accept there was a measure of madness in her.

A very pleasant half hour passed before they rose for their drive around the plantation. "It's very bright this afternoon—'' Gilly stopped abruptly to announce, just as they were walking to the 4WD. "I think I'll stay here if you don't mind.''

Bronte who was about to slip into the back seat, snapped around, her face full of concern. "What's the matter, Gilly? Flashing lights in your eyes again?''

"Nothing to worry about, love,'' Gilly said. "They come and they go. I have to take a little more care in the sunlight these days than I used to.''

"Are you sure you're all right, Gilly?'' Steven asked. "We can cancel.''

"For heaven's sake, I won't hear of it.'' Gilly's answer was firm. "I'm sure Leo's time is limited. This is only an inconvenience of age. I'll be waiting for you when you get back.''

"I'll stay,'' Bronte said.

For answer Gilly threw out an arm. "Go *now*, ducky!" she ordered. "I'm as right as rain."

"Well then, ma'am." Steven saluted her. "We're off! Shouldn't be long."

Several times along the way they left the vehicle parked in the shade while Leo strode around the beautiful lush landscape, his movements so animated, his expression so intense he might have been planning the future job in his head. He seemed captivated with the fringing rain forest waving to them as he stomped off as though it was an imperative to take a private view.

"Where did you two meet?" Bronte asked.

"I've known Leo since forever," Steven answered, watching the landscape designer disappear into the dense line of trees.

"I thought you had one or two bad moments when Leo recognised me."

He glanced down at her. Butterflies in a myriad of colours were fluttering around them, full of nectar from the prolifically blossoming lantana near the rain forest fringe. To his fascination one alighted on the bare satiny skin of her shoulder, beautiful sapphire blue and black wings folded.

"Whatever made you think that?" he asked very softly.

Bronte stood as still as a statue not wanting the butterfly to flutter away though a dozen and more of its mates, some with brilliant green and black wings were hovering in the vicinity. "I'm keeping a pretty good eye on you," she whispered. "Randolph's not your real name is it?" It was nothing more than a wild hunch but she decided to play it.

"It certainly is. It's my legal name." He held out a finger to the exquisite butterfly but it flew away. "Damn!"

"You scared it off. Anyway Leo will tell me."

His clear green eyes gleamed like a big cat's. "How *could* you think of speaking to Leo behind my back? What could he possibly tell you, you silly girl?" he lifted her long dark hair away from her cheek, holding it like a silk scarf. "I'm leading a double life?"

"*Are* you?" She dared not turn up her face to him. His touch, grazing her nape, was a delicious agony she had to brace herself against. "Why are you estranged from your family?" she asked with some urgency because she really wanted to know.

"Bronte, aren't you estranged from yours?" he countered. "Don't we both have the right to live our own lives?"

Bronte understood this very well, still she said: "Not if you're not using your correct name?"

His laugh had a slight edge. "What's next on the agenda, Interpol? What in hell has it got to do with anything we're doing here? I told you my father and I don't get on. *Big time!* I have a duty to love him and I tried, but my father's not accustomed to loving people. He scores better hating them. It happens with some fathers and sons. My mother is dead and I don't get on particularly well with my brother, either. My father has been a tremendous influence on him. Not me! Believe me that's a strong incentive to get as far away as possible."

"Does Leo know your father?" she asked carefully, staring into his handsome face.

"Don't take it upon yourself to ask him. I'll tell you myself, he does."

"Does Leo like your father?" The butterflies were still hovering, the sun gleaming off the brilliant patterns and spots of iridescent colour.

He regarded their flight for a moment in silence. "The alpha and omega of Leo's life is landscape gardening. It's a passion with him. It would do you no good at all, Bronte, to ask Leo questions about my family. He wouldn't *dream* of telling you anything."

"Then obviously there's a great deal to tell," Bronte said. "Your father sounds like he rules the roost."

"Like Brandt. Doesn't he?" Steven retaliated. "These guys get so big they think they're outside the law."

Inexplicably Bronte took that minute to defend her stepfather. "Are you trying to say my stepfather is a criminal?"

Steven's shapely mouth compressed. "I think he spends a good deal of time bypassing the rules and regulations. Integrity gets lost along the way."

Bronte couldn't argue with that. She bowed her head. "Look, I'm not trying to invade your precious privacy. It's a matter of being able to trust you—"

"With *your* inheritance?" His question cut her off.

"With Gilly's *life!*" She erupted, like a small volcano. "I'm just not as trusting as she is. She thinks you're going to work wonders."

Answering anger lit his eyes. "I am! I guarantee it. I like to aim high."

"Goodness, you're sure of yourself, aren't you?" She made a tiny adjustment to the sarong skirt that flowed silkily around her slender, supple form.

"Why not?" His eyes followed her graceful movements, so for a moment he couldn't get a grasp on what he was saying. "The very fact Leo has consented to come here and perhaps draw up plans suggests a man of his calibre is ready to trust me."

"Yes, it does," she admitted.

"Would you mind repeating that?" he asked sarcastically.

"I will not. You heard the first time."

"Is there no way you can lay down your prickly armour?" He looked down at her. "You're not an easy woman to deal with. I'm sorry if I refuse to be drawn into a discussion about my family. They're irrelevant to whatever dealings we have."

"Perhaps, but I happen to think it seems like evasion."

His eyes taunted, tantalised, challenged. "Do you feel like talking about how you called off the wedding that everyone wanted?"

"Everyone except me," she cried, moving out of the chink of sunlight that trickled through the foliage.

"So why did you wait so long?" He studied her flush, the lack of composure.

"None of your business."

"Aah!" He let out a long breath. "Then why don't you keep your pretty nose out of mine? I appreciate you want to check on me as Gilly's *business* partner. I have a suggestion. Why don't we call on Chika Moran at Wildwood one day? He's another one of my partners. We can see if he's happy with the way things are going and if he's happy with *me*."

She lifted her long hair like a sail, exposing her slender, vulnerable looking neck. "I like to keep as far away as I can from crocs."

"And very wise, too. Hippos are more dangerous but we don't have any at the park. I'm not suggesting you give Chika and the boys a hand. Have you ever been to Wildwood?"

She nodded, her skin crawling with an involuntary shudder. Even so crocodiles had their own repulsive fascination as the wild life parks had learned fast. "Gilly took me. It really was *wild* wood then. It's not normal to share the garden paths with salties out for a stroll."

He laughed. "They're okay if you don't get between them and where they want to go. Also you never, never invade *their* territory. Apart from that, they're reasonably well behaved for prehistoric creatures. They don't normally attack without provocation."

"That's good to know. They just frighten you to death, fearsome creatures. They might look like they lumber along on their short legs but they're unbelievably fast. I've seen them slip down their runways into the water."

"I assure you they're all fenced off now."

"So who mows the enclosures, you?" she asked sarcastically, stepping further back into the shade of a massive banyan tree whose bulk had withstood the fiercest cyclones. As she did so she saw Leo Marsdon emerging from the forest.

"Haven't you been hearing a word I've told you? Chika or one of his sons do that. Are you scared to come?"

Scared? That was the last straw! "I am *not*," she burst out. It had a lot to do with the way she was feeling, half hostile, half out of control. "I wasn't scared then and I'm not now. I'm game."

"Great!" A tiny bud of flame danced in his eyes. "What about early next week? We can have lunch at the Lodge then take a run out to Wildwood. You know all about the Queensland amethyst python. They've got a few twenty feet or more. If you were really as game as you say I could arrange a trip to the Gulf before the Wet sets in. We could go out on a tidal river and do a bit of filming of the wild life, see the mighty saurian at work and play."

"Are you serious?" She felt impelled to stare into his face. His light eyes were startling against his deep tan. She sucked in her breath as all her senses stirred.

"So help me, I am!" There was a sensuous twist to his mouth.

"Are you saying the two of us go off together?"

"Wouldn't you feel safe?" he asked.

His eyes seemed to be drawing her into him. She had to shake her head to clear it. "No, I would not. You could well take it into your head to toss me in the river."

He laughed. "I think even a crocodile would think twice about tangling with you, Bronte. We can ask Gilly to come along as a chaperone if you like. We've left it too late to start on any major work if our project goes ahead. All builders cease operations at the beginning of December. They won't start up again until the worst of the Wet is over. I suggest we do something about your access road as soon as possible. We haven't had a bad cyclone for years now, but chances are they'll start up again. That track will turn to impassable mud."

"Don't I know it. You're not looking to Gilly, I hope, to mortgage Oriole if you can't raise all the finance for your project? If that happens, I'll tell you right now I can persuade Gilly to call the whole thing off.''

His handsome features tautened. ''You know, Bronte, you're right to worry I might have a little something lined up for you. Gilly knows perfectly well mortgaging Oriole was never part of the deal. She puts up Oriole. My job is to turn it into a beautiful rain forest retreat.''

''It cheers me to hear you say it!'' Bronte couldn't withhold the sarcasm from her voice. ''Forgive me, if I've offended you.''

''That's fine. Really. Your being bitchy is like water off a duck's back. Oh look, here's Leo returning. I bet he's got lots of ideas.''

CHAPTER SIX

AT THE end of the week Bronte and Gilly drove into town to meet Steven and sign the joint venture agreement drawn up by Gilly's solicitor Maurice Meiklejohn of Meiklejohn and Meiklejohn who on Bronte's reckoning, had to be around in the days when the dinosaurs were fighting their fierce battles. Mr. Maurice Meiklejohn didn't come into the office every day they were informed by a secretary, something Bronte didn't find at all surprising, but as his father before him had personally acted for the McAllisters, Mr. Maurice wished to keep up the tradition.

Steven met them at the front of the building, an excellent small scale late 19th century commercial building with a very interesting parapet.

"All set?" He took Gilly's arm.

"Rarin' to go!" Gilly was in fine form.

"And you, Bronte?" Steven asked. "You look an absolute picture!"

"Oh shut up."

"Doesn't she, Gilly?"

Gilly's black eyes lit up with mischief. "New dress. We've had to do some shopping. Poor child had little more than the clothes she stood up in."

"And very fetching, too!" Steven let his glance slip up and down the quietly simmering Bronte. She wore a dress of the utmost simplicity, short, sleeveless, round necked in a soft, singing shade of red that, to his surprise, suited her almost as well as her favourite deep blue. It skimmed her slender body, not clinging at any point yet he was acutely aware of the very feminine contours beneath that silky slide, the allure that was largely unconscious and doubly potent because of it. Bronte McAllister he had discovered lacked the vanity many beautiful women had. If anything she was touchingly insecure which he supposed had a lot to do with her dysfunctional life.

Inside Meiklejohn and Meiklejohn's air-conditioned offices they were ushered almost immediately into the senior partner's inner sanctum. Maurice Meiklejohn rose to his inconsiderable height from behind a huge, Victorian, partners desk that dwarfed him.

"Gillian! Dear Gillian! I'm so happy to see you!" He opened his arms wide to embrace her. He was dressed in a rumpled cream linen suit that looked like he may have taken a nap in it, spotless white shirt, striped tie that he might have owned since he was a schoolboy, askew. The overall impression was one of a sweet and kindly great-grandfather, which in fact he was.

Gilly obliged. Both patted each other many times on the back much as a mother burps her baby.

Bronte had never heard anyone call her great-aunt *Gillian* in her entire life.

"You remember my little Bronte, of course?"

Dutifully Bronte stepped forward, a smile on her face. Why did Gilly always refer to her as my *little* Bronte. She was five foot eight in her heels.

"Yes, yes, I know Bronte. You couldn't prise the youngsters in the family away from the television the nights she was on. I took many a peek myself. Even so beautiful you were a very credible police woman, Bronte. I believe there were floods of tears at your violent demise?"

"I didn't know I was so popular," Bronte laughed.

"And Steven. Steven Randolph, my soon to be partner." Gilly turned to include the young man at her shoulder.

"Ah, yes, Steven." The two men shook hands, Steven terrified of breaking the old man's bones, as brittle as a bird's.

Bronte studied the tableau they presented. One so young,

so tall, so handsome and virile, the other shrunken by age with a fuzz of white hair, but for all that showing his acuity in the alertness of his gaze. "Why Steven and I have already met, Gillian," he announced. "He was very kind to me when I had a bit of a sick turn at a meeting—some environmental issue—a year or so back. Do you remember *me,* my boy?"

"Of course I do, sir, even if I never did get your name."

"I'm sorry about that. I wasn't myself that evening. I hope I thanked you properly."

"You did indeed."

Maurice Meiklejohn beamed. "Well I suppose we must get on with the business at hand. I must say, Gillian, I find it quite wonderful to think Oriole will be brought back to life. The times we had when we were young! I wasn't the rickety old fellow then I am now," he said, throwing Bronte a near sparkling glance. "And Gillian here had a whole circle of us fascinated. She had the most marvellous hair! Like yours, Bronte, a thick curtain of black satin with that same bluish lustre. Many the story I could tell you about your great-aunt."

"I'm begging you not to, Morrie," Gilly actually blushed, but moved serenely into the chair Steven held for her.

Afterwards to celebrate Steven took them all to lunch at the Lodge, Maurice Meiklejohn included. The two elderly people, seated in the back of the car, talked nonstop as if they had to fit everything in, in case they never saw one another again.

Up front Bronte and Steven maintained a silence that had at its heart a powerful, unsought attraction.

The exquisite Christine was there to greet them, showing them to a table that was quickly and efficiently reset for four.

"What a treat!" The solicitor looked happily around him. "I've heard the food is wonderful."

Gilly looked back in surprise. "Are you telling me, Morrie, you and Gwen haven't dined here?"

The solicitor laid a fond hand over hers. "You know what Gwennie's like."

"I would have hoped she'd grown out of it," Gilly replied.

"She's still jealous of you," Maurice Meiklejohn said and burst out laughing.

It turned out to be a happy reunion. The food they chose was light but delicious. Christine, dressed in another very chic outfit—lilac this time—that featured an ankle-length wrapover skirt, beautifully embroidered around the border, flitted back and forth, dainty as a butterfly, her dark eyes full of secrets, resting longingly on her business partner. Bronte had the unshakable feeling Christine was in love with him. He *had* to know. She had a sudden vision of their two heads sharing a pillow. One ebony, the other gleaming mahogany streaked with gold. It caused such a constriction in her throat for a few seconds she couldn't breathe.

Once again as they were leaving over two hours later, Christine had a private word with Steven. Gilly and Morrie walked arm in arm out the entrance. They might be past their dancing days, but they were very spry. Bronte stood fused to the spot, ostensibly admiring another spectacular arrangement of flowers featuring wonderful heads of the Bird of Paradise, streliztia. After a few moments more of seeming absorption Christine walked with Steven to where Bronte was waiting.

She smiled into Bronte's face. "I was just saying to Steven you must join us this Saturday evening. I'm having a little party at my house."

"It's her birthday." Steven smiled. A smile that would make any woman go weak at the knees.

Christine held up her pretty golden hands. "No presents," she said. "Just the pleasure of good friends. You will come, Bronte?"

"I'd be delighted to. Thank you for asking."

"Then that's settled!" Christine laid her hand briefly on Steven's arm, smiling with sweet familiarity into his face.

Of course! They're as thick as thieves, Bronte thought, cursing herself for her own intense interest.

Violent delights had violent ends. Like Gilly her love affairs were never going to end well.

Love affair? *What love affair?* It was a moment of pure shock.

I won't let this happen. I won't.

Steven unaware of all her soul searching directed her out of the cool restaurant lobby into the brilliant sunlight.

Leo Marsdon had returned to his commission further down the coast but he had promised to send them some sketches of what he envisioned for the extensive grounds, although it was his practice to work almost entirely on site. No actual work could start until after the Wet in any case, so he had time, he'd told them, if they liked his ideas to come up with something really worthwhile. Splendid trees of immense height were already growing on the estate. What he wanted to do was create several ornamental lagoons—at the same time expanding the already existing natural spring and introducing water birds in particular the native black swan. He also suggested a track encircling their volcanic plug where walkers or horse riders could enjoy the beauties of the tropical landscape. A lot of machinery would have to be brought in, he'd warned them, looking straight at Gilly—bulldozers, excavators, backhoes etc. But he could foresee spectacular results. What's more he gave every indication he might handle the commission himself instead of passing it over to a colleague.

Gilly was thrilled! Every morning she greeted Bronte wreathed in smiles. The sky was bluer than ever. The sun more golden. Even the heat was bearable.

On the Saturday night as Bronte stood staring at herself in the mirror, Gilly knocked on the door. Bronte called, ''Come in. I'm near ready.''

"Oh, don't you look gorgeous!" Gilly entered, clasping her hands together as she circled Bronte's slender figure.

Bronte saw herself no such way. Inside she was churning with conflicting emotions. They buffeted her this way and that, like a kayak in white water. "You always tell me that, Gilly. You told me I looked gorgeous when I was twelve and allowed to go to a school dance. I remember the dress. It was a sari you discovered in an old box and made into a party dress. All the kids made fun of me and asked me if I was a Hindu."

"With those blue eyes! That's when we first found out you look lovely in red. At least your dress has splashes of red roses and leaves. You've picked up a light tan. The white goes well against it."

"Do you think it's nice enough?" Bronte asked, turning side-on to get another angle.

"Don't be silly! Of course it's nice enough. What's bothering you, child?"

"Christine is sure to look wonderful."

"She's a very beautiful lady but she won't outshine you." Gilly continued her leisurely inspection of her great-niece. "You know she's in love with him?"

Bronte couldn't help herself. She nodded glumly.

Gilly laid an arm around her shoulder and squeezed. "I knew you fancied him."

"I do *not!*"

"If only you did." Gilly smiled. "There's a man who could make you happy. If only you'd stop being rude to him."

"Rude? I'm not rude. A bit brusque, maybe, but not *rude.*"

"Not that it's a real problem," Gilly considered. "I think he sees through you."

"I'd much prefer to be inscrutable. Do you think I should leave my hair down or put it up?"

"It's perfect the way it is. You know what Morrie said about *my* hair when I was young. Men love long hair."

"What a nice man Morrie is," Bronte said.

"He'd talk the hind leg off a donkey."

Bronte laughed aloud. "*You* should talk! Surely it's about time Mrs. Meiklejohn trusts him with you?"

"Never!" Gilly said with deep satisfaction. "I was very hotly desired in my day. An object of passion you might say, but I'd gained a bit of a reputation for being *difficult*. Don't let that happen to you, my girl."

"Maybe it's in the genes, Gilly," Bronte said, a shade ruefully.

"Don't be silly. You have the blood of pioneers in your veins, pioneers who built our nation. Visionaries. Adventurers. You, young Bronte, are descended from a long line of splendid, courageous McAllisters." Gilly declared, with a flourish of her arms.

"Maybe I'm the last in the line?"

Gilly looked at her great-niece bracingly. "Well if you are, it'll be your own silly fault. Now I can hear Steven coming up the drive. You get out there and enjoy yourself. That's an order."

"You'd have made a good general yourself!" Bronte gave Gilly an exaggerated salute. She turned to take one last look in the mirror, aware of the quickened beating of her heart. To slow it she reminded herself this wasn't a date. He was simply doing her a favour driving her to Christine's birthday party. She wasn't going empty-handed. She didn't like that idea no matter what Christine had said. She'd settled on a gift pack of champagne with two crystal flutes as appropriate for the occasion.

In one graceful sweep Bronte picked up her lovely designer evening bag—previous owner, Miranda—then gave Gilly a quick kiss on the cheek. "I love you, you old battleaxe," she said sweetly. "Don't wait up for me."

"I won't need to worry," Gilly assured her. She followed

Bronte out the door, catching wafts of the lovely perfume she was wearing. "Not when you're with Steven."

"Where exactly does Christine live?" Bronte asked, when they were five minutes into the journey.

"Pandanus Point." He named a well-known beauty spot overlooking the Coral Sea.

"But that's where *you* live!" She had seen his address on the Joint Venture contract.

"Does that worry you?" He glanced at her, thinking she looked too beautiful for words.

"Of course not!" She averted her head, staring out the window at the shimmering landscape. The moon was at its full. An enormous, languorous copper moon that lit up the earth. "I haven't been there for years."

"You wouldn't know it," he said. "There's been a good bit of development going on. Calypso Enterprises developed a site of about thirty acres. They met with opposition from a few locals who didn't want anyone else there but themselves and others who were concerned it would cause environmental problems. As it turned out Calypso did a marvellous job and everyone calmed down. There are regulations in place governing the sort of house one can build there. No one can block anyone else's view. Designs have to be submitted to council to ensure the buildings fit into the environment. It's quite beautiful, really. There are similar houses on the Hawaiian islands. Christine and I got in on the ground floor. We're only five minutes away from each other."

"Handy." She should have known better than to say it, but she did.

"Well there's that. We're partners. Living close by makes it simple to discuss things. It hasn't been easy for Christine trying to overcome her grief but I think she's much happier up here. She's kept busy and doesn't have time to brood. Running the restaurant, meeting so many people, she's been able to make new friends."

"Well she's an artist at what she does," Bronte said quite sincerely. "Is it possible to have a quick peep at your modest abode?"

"I'm thrilled you want to see it," he said smoothly.

"A house can say a lot about a person," Bronte observed.

"So how could we describe Oriole homestead?"

She had to smile. "Eclectic—isn't that an awful word to say?—eccentric, haunted, half-hidden in the jungle, nestling beneath a miniature volcanic mountain, overflowing with colour, saturated with a million fragrances, swept by tropical breezes. Do you want me to go on?"

"Better not. You were putting me to sleep. We're going to make Paradise of it, Bronte."

"It's Paradise already," she shot back.

"In a manner of speaking but it was fast turning into a lost world with Gilly trapped inside. I'm sure even Adam and Eve had to have clear outs."

She bowed her head. "I'm being ungracious."

"Never!" he said.

"All right, you *have* done a lot for Gilly. She appreciates it. She thinks you're great."

"You obviously don't."

"I'm not about to stroke your ego, Steven."

"I can hardly contain my disappointment, but it's very nice the way you say *Steven.*"

Christine's house was as special as she was. It was built on high land overlooking the sea, a startlingly blue by day, tonight aglitter with the moon's broad rays.

"I like that!" Bronte said looking up at the single-storey home.

"A relative of Christine's designed it. He's a brilliant young architect who lives and works in Singapore."

"Which accounts for its elegant Asian character. You're not adjacent?" her eyes shifted to the beautiful house beside it, all lit up.

"That house belongs to the Nicols. You'll be meeting them tonight. I'm further down. We can take a look afterwards."

Which mightn't be a sensible idea after all, Bronte thought, sucking in her breath.

There were a number of cars parked outside, around the paved cul de sac and on the grass of a small park opposite the avenue of generously spaced houses.

Christine met them at the door, her appearance in a long close-fitting Chinese cheongsam in embossed jade silk as captivating as ever. As she introduced them to everyone she held onto Steven's arm. A little to her discomfort Bronte found herself instantly recognised as her TV character. It was a hop, step and a jump to the fact she'd jilted media magnate Richard Saunders's son Nathan though no one was crass enough to comment on that.

Bronte found herself drawn aside by a very attractive man, maybe early forties, who had honed in on her beauty from the moment she'd walked through the door. His name was Guy Butler. He had a wide generous smile and fine grey-green eyes. For some reason he thought Bronte would love talking about herself—her stalled TV career, but that was the last thing she wanted. She would have much preferred to arrive incognito but it came out in the course of conversation Christine had given her guests prior knowledge she would be joining the party.

Just as Guy Butler was overwhelming her with his attention, Steven came to her rescue. "Sorry to break in," he said smoothly, not looking sorry at all, "but I'd like to show Bronte the house. She loved it from the outside and the inside is just as good."

"We'll catch up again, Bronte," Guy Butler promised, his eyes moving over her body rather lecherously, Bronte thought.

"I'd steer clear of him," Steven murmured as they walked

away. "He's looking for a new wife. That lucky woman will be Number 3."

"She most definitely won't be me," Bronte said dryly. "He must be twice my age."

"He is but he's rich and most women find him charming. The sad thing is he can't be faithful."

"Is there a man who can?"

"Bronte, you're so cynical!" He tutted, stopping a waiter to take two glasses of champagne off the tray. He passed the first to Bronte.

"To you!" He raised his glass. "You look ravishing!"

"Thank you." She stood there sipping at the deliciously cold champagne while heat swept through her lower body, down her legs, to her toes. She was sizzling! What did he think he was doing looking at her like that? It wasn't with pure and simple lust like Guy Butler, it was—what was it? Whatever it was she'd have to get over it.

"Mind the glass," he said.

"I wasn't going to drop it." She was mortified.

"I thought you were." He smiled, taking her by the elbow and steering her through the small crowd to the rear terrace overlooking the sea. The open plan living-dining room was large, the areas defined by richly polished teak columns and carved arches to walk under. The furnishings were minimal. Extraordinarily so when compared with Oriole's jostle Bronte thought. There were a few superb Chinese antique pieces that looked to be of museum quality. They drew the eye but didn't detract from the main purpose, the architect's interior design. The rear wall was entirely of glass framed by the same carved timber arches to take full advantage of the spectacular view. It wasn't a big house—after all only Christine lived there— but it was as beautiful and elegant as she was.

Christine didn't leave them alone for very long. She found them enjoying the sea breezes and the spectacle of the full moon's golden rays on the water.

"*St-e-ven!*" The charming lisp, the dazzling, enigmatic

smile. "There you are! Frank Corelli's arrived. He's asking for you," she lowered her voice. "He's an important man to have on side. I can take care of Bronte, not that she needs taking care of. Everyone is very impressed with her."

Especially when you told them all to be on the lookout, Bronte thought, but naturally could not say.

"I'll go then," Steven said. "Maybe you both could join us in about ten minutes?"

"We will," Christine promised.

They both stood watching him walk away. His lightweight beige jacket hugged his wide shoulders. His walk was confident, graceful, athletic, head carried high.

"He's a wonderful looking man, isn't he?" Christine said, and graced Bronte with a sidelong smile. "He interests you?"

"I barely know him," Bronte said, hoping she hadn't changed colour under that piercing regard.

Christine looked back at her with a flicker of what could have been *contempt?* Surely not. "That actually doesn't mean anything. Attraction is instant, is that not so?"

"Well as you said, he's an extremely attractive man," Bronte answered, defensively. "However, it's the quiet life I'm looking for. One reason why I'm here."

"And how long will you be staying?" Christine asked, holding back her black spun silk hair so the breeze stroked her nape. "I expect you are looking forward to returning to your TV work." She made a pretty gesture towards the living room where the melange of people were talking and laughing, enjoying themselves. "You have a lot of fans in there."

"I'm afraid I got on the wrong side of the man who owns the channel," Bronte said.

"Ah, yes." Christine gave her a knowing look. "For a man like that public humiliation would be difficult if not impossible to take. But then, you're so *young* that explains it."

"Explains what?" Bronte asked. The older woman spoke

as if she was far, far wiser and probably was. Still Bronte
was a McAllister and not about to be patronised.

"So sorry, Bronte, what am I thinking of? You are my
guest." Christine drew an apologetic hand to her breast.

"Why did you invite me, Christine?" Bronte tackled the
question head-on.

"Whatever do you mean?" For an instant the inscrutabil-
ity was gone. There was a flicker of hostility in the brilliant
black eyes. "I wish to be friendly. Steven and Miss
McAllister are now partners in what I know will be a successful venture. You are Miss McAllister's great-niece and it
is right I offer hospitality."

She sounded shocked, but Bronte knew intuitively it was
just an act. "Well I'm sorry if I offended you," Bronte said.
"Trust me, I'm not about to become involved with Steven
Randolph if that's what you want to know?"

Christine stared back as though she couldn't believe her
ears. "You are so direct. You Australians, so direct."

"We don't beat about the bush, no," Bronte said. "I understand perfectly you're interested in Steven yourself."

Christine visibly swallowed and put a hand to her throat.
"I have lost my husband not all that long ago."

"I'm deeply sorry for you," Bronte said and meant it. "I
know all about loss, but maybe a little light has come into
your life again?" Her voice softened even though she knew
Christine didn't like her.

"We don't plan these things." Christine sounded a little
agitated as though the conversation wasn't going to plan.
"Steven came into my life when I was at a very low ebb.
He has been very kind to me. Many men are not kind as
you've learned to your cost. We're partners and each day we
grow closer. Steven must be given time to know what he
really wants."

Meanwhile you hold him with bonds of silk. "But *you*
already know?" Bronte asked, not worrying about her *di-*

rectness. After all, Christine had initiated the whole tone of the conversation.

"Our bond of friendship has given me great happiness," Christine said, her gaze locking almost hypnotically on Bronte's. "Maybe there is something more in store for us? Who knows?"

I shouldn't have come here. I should go home, Bronte thought, as some fraught moments later they walked back into the living room. Christine was so petite, so doll-like, she must look like a brolga, Bronte thought. Steven being so tall she'd worn stilettos that night. She knew perfectly well Christine didn't like her, not so much personally perhaps, but as a perceived threat. Women were like that.

It had been a mistake. She'd known from the moment she saw Steven and Christine together, Steven was terribly important to Christine. Not only as a business partner. She had come to lean on him. Not that she blamed Christine for wanting more. Steven Randolph had enough charisma to turn any woman on. But surely there were quite a few years between them? Ten, more? less? Not that it mattered all that much. Christine was *ageless*. A porcelain figure with perfectly preserved skin.

They said their goodbyes just after midnight although they were the first guests to leave. Most lived in the area but Steven and Bronte had the trip back to Oriole in front of them. Guy Butler followed them to the door—he had near glued himself to Bronte's side all night—whispering to her he'd give her a ring like she was going to cry buckets if he didn't.

"He wants us to 'do' lunch," Bronte explained to an enquiring Steven on the way to the car.

"How many wives does a man really want?" Steven mused. "How long does he stay with one before he's ready to move on to another? I think the last marriage went on the rocks after eighteen months."

"That's hardly a record." Bronte sniffed. "I know a bride-groom who refused to go home with his bride."

"You're joking." Steven opened the door for her.

"I am not. I was one of the bridesmaids. They had a dread-ful fight at the reception. He claimed he was saved from a life of misery. She told everyone he was gay."

"Was he?"

"I have no idea whatsoever."

Inside the car Bronte had to battle the spiralling excitement that plagued her every moment she was with him. "I think we should go straight home," she announced.

His laugh was incredulous. "You sound like a teenager out on her first date. I'm not planning a seduction scene. I genuinely want to show you my house."

"You can show me another time."

"What is it? What's bothering you? Something is, I've been sensing it all night."

"To be honest, I found Guy Butler absolutely stunning. I don't know that I'm prepared to offer myself to him as wife number three. You're going the wrong way."

"Settle down, Bronte," he lightly jeered. "You'll never come to any harm with me."

"You mean we can't have an affair?" She gave an elab-orate sigh.

"No. Despite your shortcomings you're the sort of girl a guy would want to marry."

Strangely enough she'd found it to be true. "Affairs are much easier. We could both go on our way afterwards and there always is an afterwards, men being what they are. I'm not a virginal little teenager, either. I had a fiancé, I thought I loved him."

Steven felt like doing something drastic to Nat Saunders. "Put on your seat belt," he said.

"What?" It wasn't the retort she expected.

"Strap yourself in. It's the law."

She shot him a withering look. "It's the middle of the

night. We're on an empty, near-private road. Okay.'' She strapped herself in only to unstrap herself a few moments later as they pulled into his driveway.

She saw him smile.

''Having fun?''

''It's been a lovely evening. And it's not over.''

''I strongly advise against the seduction scene,'' she warned lightly. ''I don't want it to get around but I'm very unpredictable. I do things like pulling out of a wedding at the last minute.''

''That doesn't count as a crime,'' he told her smoothly. ''And it wasn't unpredictable, it was *smart*. Come in.''

She was out of the car before he reached her, looking up at his house. ''Excuse me, you live here all by *yourself?*'' Christine's house was a doll's house compared to this.

''You're not going to lecture me, are you? I have a cleaning lady who comes in twice a week. A gardener about the same. I wanted a big house because one of these days I'm going to get married and have lots of children.''

''Really? I'm curious. How many? This place looks capable of housing the entire local school. What a mystery man you are. It must have cost a fortune to build?'' She frowned darkly.

He took her arm, murmuring into her ear. ''Have you never heard of bank loans?''

''I'm darn sure a bank would knock *me* back.''

''How come you always look a million dollars?'' he lightly mocked her.

''My mother's handouts plus the fact I did have a promising career now gone with the wind.''

''Do you miss it?'' He sounded serious.

''Strangely enough, no. Early morning calls. Changing scripts at the last minute. Getting kicked out.''

''I don't know how many times I replayed that last episode,'' he confessed. ''Maybe I fell just a little in love with you then.'' Steven produced a key from the depths of a pocket and inserted it in the front door. "Welcome to my modest abode."

"How truly deceptive you are." Bronte entered the house very quietly as though Christine down the avenue could hear her. "Most men have to wait until they're fifty and well and truly arrived before they can afford a house like this. In fact I think it's high time you settled down and started that family."

"It's not as if I asked you." He gave her a sardonic smile.

Even from the front door, a carved double door, the sparkling blue sea would always be in view. The tropical sunsets would be glorious.

"You're going to be hugely in demand when your women suitors see this," she remarked, looking around her with the greatest interest "I like this very much. It's *you*."

"What an admission." He jeered. "Could you say that again?"

"All that champagne has gone to my head. Besides, I can't bother to repeat myself."

Steven followed her as she wandered across the living room. He'd had it decorated in different tones of white and palest cream. Some marvellous old stone capitals he'd bought at an antique sale a few years back in Sydney served as side tables. They were a great touch he always thought. The custom made sofas and armchairs he'd had covered in hand-woven fabrics.

"Eastern influences haven't spilled in here," Bronte remarked, her eyes moving slowly from one thing to another. "It's classic with a modern update." A few very good large paintings hung on the walls, landscapes of intense colours that would stand up to the spectacular daytime view. It was a great house she decided. Masculine but not off-putting to females. Strong lines. Classical feel. Confident.

"What's the verdict?"

"Very accomplished," she said.

"Thank you for that."

"Of course not every woman wants a dozen children. A dozen okay?" she turned her head over her shoulder, her blue-violet eyes conveying a taunt.

He was closer than she thought. "I don't bring many women here, Bronte. This is my sanctuary like Oriole's yours."

"All the same I could be comfortable here. Turn on a few more lights," she said, in no frame of mind to be so *alone* with him in this still, seductive half light. Only a thought occurred to her. "No, don't!"

That caught him by surprise.

"I don't want anyone to know I'm here."

"Why ever not?"

"It's a hostile world out there," she said, waving her hand about vaguely. "Oh, you have an infinity pool?" She changed the subject, catching sight of the glimmering sheet of water.

"Come for a swim one day," he invited.

A current of heat went through her at the expression in his eyes. "Your house couldn't be more different to Christine's."

"Is that so surprising?" He moved steadily nearer.

"Just an observation. You had an architect?"

"I drew up my own plans," Steven told her. "I had a good friend—a *real* architect vet them. There wasn't a lot he changed. I suppose you could say it was a collaboration."

"It's a pity you couldn't have followed your dream," she said, feeling as though she was being pulled towards him with invisible fingers.

"At nearly thirty I find it extraordinary that I didn't. At seventeen I was just a boy. I toed the line."

"I know what that means," she said wryly. "For me it was more like buckling under." They were talking quietly, yet the atmosphere was so taut it could have shattered like glass. Bronte tried to concentrate on the elements of design, the textures, the polished stone, the great areas of glass, but it was impossible to absorb anything when he was standing only a few feet from her with the knowledge he could dominate her.

It was her own fault. She'd come into this with her eyes wide-open. It was up to her to get herself out. She turned to him, and her eyes flashed pure sapphire. "I'd love to come back another time. In daylight." She tried to adopt a bright yet casual tone, but it was difficult when her emotions at that point were chaotic.

"I can almost hear your heart racing," he said gently. "It's okay, Bronte. I'm not asking for anything you don't want to give."

"I'm not sure I believe that." She swallowed on a dry throat. She had to get more distance between them. Delicately she sidestepped him, her conversation with Christine weighing heavily on her mind.

"What are you so nervous about?" he asked. "It's not like we're on a date."

"I just think I should move to a safer location as soon as possible," she said. "We mightn't be on a date but we've been dancing around each other all night."

"Maybe we have a special affinity?" He reached out unexpectedly, caught her hand.

She found herself looking deep into his eyes. "Maybe, but I can assure you I don't have sex on my mind."

"Well, *I* do!" His voice came to her, deep, low, faintly wry. "You're so challenging, Bronte. But I like it like that."

Slowly he turned her into his arms, the flush on her creamy cheeks reflecting the heat in her blood. She started to speak. Stopped. There seemed little she could do but yield to the pressure of desire.

"I love your perfume," he murmured, bending to kiss her on the sensitive skin beneath her ear. "What is it?"

"Me. Bronte McAllister," she whispered, making a tiny halfhearted attempt to break away. "And a little gardenia."

"It's beautiful. You're beautiful. Kiss me, Bronte McAllister."

Goose bumps ran down her arms. Sensation enveloped her like a cloud. "You really want it so much?"

"Yes," he breathed.

"Just once."

She rose to him on tiptoes. Their lips touched. She kept her mouth rounded in a pucker, lips closed.

That lasted the briefest time. Waves of desire shot through her as she felt the exquisite touch of his tongue. It parted her lips gently, found its way into her open mouth. He was tasting her, running the tip of his tongue across the porcelain of her teeth. She could feel her breasts swelling, the nipples going painfully taut.

He pulled her in closer, recognising her arousal. He reciprocated in full measure. The kiss went on and on. Bronte didn't know how long. Didn't care. It was rapturous. Without exerting any pressure, he was drawing from her a sensational response. She had to break the kiss to breathe, gasping for air, but his mouth continued its sensuous trail down across her chin to the curve of her throat. "Don't pull away, Bronte," he muttered as she made the slightest movement. "Please…no!"

The note—near anguish in his voice—caused tears to spurt. It all had an aura of unreality. A dream. Now her little gasps of yearning were audible in the golden gloom. It was impossible to breathe normally. Surely this was everything she ever wanted yet she said: "Steven, we should leave."

"I know." He knew he was spinning out of control yet he continued to kiss her. Her face and throat, the hollow of her neck, her collarbone, the swell of her breasts above the low neckline of her dress. Desire unlike anything he had ever known had its grip on him.

She too was frantic for those kisses to alight on her mouth.

Her legs were trembling so much she thought she would lose balance. She had to lean into him, their bodies joined at the hip and the thigh, his legs spread a little to accommodate hers pressing against him so she was exquisitely aware of the strength of his arousal. "This won't solve anything." Even so it was worth it.

"What do you want solved?" He bent her back a little so he could look into her eyes.

"I've made a big enough mess of my life. Business and pleasure don't mix."

"With *you* they mix perfectly." His voice was a husky whisper.

The touch of his mouth on hers was *stunning*. She moaned from the pleasure and thought it had to be like being under the influence of a powerful aphrodisiac. Hearing nothing. Caring for nothing but sensation. His hand sought her breast, shaped it through the thin material, lifted it higher in his palm. His other arm slid down her back, following the curves and cleavages of her body. Bronte knew where this was going but she couldn't seem to *put* an end to it. She wanted to abandon herself entirely, to lie with him in a bed where her hunger could be assuaged. She wanted his hands and his mouth on her naked flesh. She wanted him to *fill* her. Fill the bottomless emotional void that was in her.

"Bronte, you're crying?" He was lifting her face to him, his voice taut with concern.

She was in imminent danger of allowing him to do whatever he liked with her. "Oh, you know…women cry. It's nothing special." Her voice was brittle, not her own.

"It's special to me." His voice soothed her. He lowered his head to kiss the tear drops off her cheeks, tasting salt. "Did I frighten you? I didn't mean to come on so strong." He realized he was losing sight of everything, but *her* and how much he wanted her.

"You're a frightening guy." She managed a little laugh.

"Because I want you? You already know that. I'm sure I've wanted you from the moment I saw you. Sandalled feet planted so firmly on the bush track, all hostile and suspicious, ready for a confrontation." He held her shoulders. "I can't seem to let go of you." This was something radically new for him. He was the guy who liked to be in control.

"You'll have to. I have to go home, Steven. I'd started a new life. I'd sworn off men."

"You haven't sworn off being made love to," he retorted. "You're as attracted to me as I am to you. I think we've proved that. I want you, Bronte. I want you in my bed. Above all, I want you to trust me."

"Serious wants." She finally had the strength back in her legs. She pulled away. "I know men can handle a couple of women at a time. I know how quickly they go from one to another. The most beautiful women in the world can't seem to hold on to their men. Me? I have my pride."

"Pride?" He reached for her again, not fiercely but with the gesture of a man who would go to great lengths to make her care.

"Oh, Steven, I—"

Whatever she was going to say was cut short by the din of the main phone and the various extension phones ringing through the large house.

"Who the devil could that be at this hour?" Steven looked and sounded impatient of the distraction.

"Don't answer it," Bronte said, with a warning shake of her head. "It's your partner checking up on you."

"Christine?" His green eyes glittered. "Don't be ridiculous."

"I'm not the one who's being ridiculous." Bronte began her move to the front door. "Whether you believe me or not, I have powers."

"Well that might explain what you do to me, but Christine would never ring me at this hour. Besides, she knows I'm driving you back to the plantation."

"Exactly!" Bronte stood her ground. "Answer it if you like. A better idea might be to take me home."

"What the hell, someone might be in trouble." He strode away.

Bronte groaned. She would put money on her hunch.

He returned a few moments later, his expression faintly irritated.

"Well?" Bronte raised an arched brow.

"I don't want to encourage you with your 'powers' but yes, that was Christine."

"Told you!"

He joined her at the door. "She was just checking whether it was me who'd turned on the lights. She saw them from her place."

"And her mind immediately sprang to burglary? Even though you've got a state-of-the-art security system?"

"She just wanted to be sure," Steven said, steering Bronte by the elbow out the door.

CHAPTER SEVEN

STEVEN lost no time having the bush track that led to the homestead sealed. It was a temporary inconvenience that left them isolated for some days but the end result would be an enormous advantage in the Wet. Bronte continued her cataloguing of the homestead's furnishings in the process turning up some amazing finds while Gilly spent hours in the huge old laundry adjoining the kitchen making up her creams and potions for a whole string of loyal customers. From time to time she wandered into the dining room where Bronte had taken up residence placing a dollop of something on Bronte's hand or arm.

"What *is* it?" Bronte asked, briskly rubbing the cream in.

"What's it look like, girl? It's hand cream, body cream, whatever you like. Forget your fancy names and outrageous prices. This'll do the trick."

"Needs a bit of perfume," Bronte suggested.

"Just as good unscented. Better." Gilly said haughtily, already on her way back to the laundry.

"Come up with something to banish wrinkles," Bronte called after her. And really, if anyone could do it, it would be Gilly.

Only all the birds in the garden, the lorikeets, the cockatoos, the galahs, the fairy wrens, the honeyeaters and the brilliant parrots were to be witness to a tired and dusty youngster's arrival at Oriole. A taxi had let Max off at the start of the broad track that led to the plantation, the driver commenting on the road works, well in progress despite the searing heat.

"And about time, too! Someone must have convinced the

old lady it needed to be done. Marooned she is in the Wet,''
he shouted as he pulled away.

Max now faced the long walk to the plantation, keeping
of necessity to the long grass at the side, hoping desperately
he wasn't about to tread on a snake. Snakes struck fear into
most people's hearts. Bronte would be amazed to see him.
He hadn't told her he was coming. Couldn't. He had made
his plans in secret. He'd had ample time on his long two
thousand mile journey from Sydney to reflect on the hide-
ousness of his position. Defying his father! His mother
wouldn't be anywhere near as bad as she was, if his father
suddenly dropped dead. It flashed through Max's mind how
often he daydreamed about pushing his father off the roof of
Brandt office tower. He was never going to be able to please
him. Not ever! He would never have survived without
Bronte, who had always tried to protect him even when his
physically threatening father had bellowed at her to ''keep
out of it!''

Bronte was very brave. A survivor. Their mother had near
abandoned her at the ripe old age of seven. Any other girl
would have slashed her wrists at what she'd had to endure
from his parents after she cancelled her wedding to that
pompous son of a bitch, Nathan Saunders. The wedding was
really to gratify his father's deep seated obsession to consol-
idate his position in society when money wasn't enough. His
father had a lot of enemies. Unfortunately not a one of them
was game to gun him down like in the movies. The bigger
the closet criminal the more they sought respectability, Max
thought.

His blood was boiling. It was *hot!*

He didn't know how much further he could go. He was so
tired. The very afternoon school broke up he hopped on a
bus to the Queensland-New South Wales border, looking he
supposed like a terrified rabbit. Another bus to Brisbane. The
tilt train to the tropical North. He thought he was covering
his tracks. He'd left a letter for his mother explaining what

he'd done. *Begging* her to intercede with his father about letting him stay with Bronte for the holidays. Bronte was the only person on earth who truly loved him. Come to that Bronte was the only person on earth he actually loved. She had the gift of making him feel he was good to be with, as well as clever which he *was* instead of a miserable, gutless calamity. It didn't count with his father he was near the top of his class of very bright boys. He wasn't *the* top. All the difference in the world. You had to be a *winner!*

A guy on a big noisy machine waved to him. He was surprised at the friendliness. He waved back but it took all his strength. He put a hand to his bare head. He wasn't wearing a hat—he only had his school hat anyway—he was such a dolt. His hair was a bunch of wet sticky curls. He was wearing his white dress shirt for school, neck open, sleeves rolled up, and his long grey flannel pants. He could feel the sweat running down his legs into his socks. He was sloshing along. He'd wanted to give Bronte a big surprise. Now he thought he was a fool not ringing ahead. Oriole's bush road at this stage was still in the process of being sealed. He wondered if there was a back road allowing them to get out. He wondered what Miss McAllister would think of him arriving at her place unannounced. She must be okay, Bronte adored her.

A headache was hammering behind Max's eyes. He'd had to be careful with his money so he'd cut back on eating. When a big 4WD pulled up just off to the right of him he couldn't believe his eyes. Maybe he was hallucinating. Maybe it was a mirage carved by the heat. It was bad enough to fry his brains.

A guy got out of the vehicle, a young guy, tall with a terrific physique, lucky devil. He'd never come by those shoulders and hard muscles. There was something very reassuring about him. Sort of like an explorer. He was even dressed like one. Cool!

"Hi, where are you going? Can I give you a lift?" The

cool guy spoke. Up close he knocked your eyes out he was so good-looking. Private school voice, vital not lethargic. The accent very much like his own.

"That'd be great!" For some reason Max found himself sitting down abruptly in the long wild grasses topped by a sea of flowers he thought might be buttercups. He hadn't meant to collapse. It just happened.

"Hey, you okay?" The guy reached him, pulling him to his feet, but keeping a steely supporting arm around him. "I'd say you've had a bit too much exposure to the sun. You wouldn't be Max, would you? Bronte's brother?"

Max loved him for that. Not Bronte's half brother, her brother. "In the flesh." He grinned. "Landed on their doorstep. Is it sun stroke? Is that what's wrong with me?"

The guy laughed. A real nice laugh. Friendly, not patronising a stupid kid. "You'll be okay once I get you up to the homestead. Steven Randolph by the way. Gilly and Bronte are my friends. I'm on a visit." Actually he was there to take Bronte to Wildwood, his wild life park.

"Then it's my lucky day. I was just about to pass out. Hi, Steven." They shook hands, man to man. "Sorry to be such a nuisance. There's a kid at school—not my class—called Randolph. He's supposed to be some kind of a whiz kid. Any relation?"

His newfound friend smiled. "We share a name. Here, get in." He gave Max a gentle shove into the passenger seat.

Air-conditioning, what bliss! It was as good as having an ice-block popped into his mouth. "No wonder people wind up dead in the desert!" Max exclaimed.

"The outback is dry heat like an oven. Here, we *steam*."

"I'll say! How did you know I was Max?" Max glanced sideways at his rescuer.

"Bronte has spoken of you. I thought you weren't allowed to come?"

Max snorted his contempt. "I did a bunk. I expect the cops

are after me as we speak. My father's a real bastard.'' Max no longer felt he owed his father loyalty.

"He does have that reputation,'' Steven agreed.

"You know him, do you?'' Max shot him a surprised look.

"A lot of people have followed Carl Brandt's high flying career,'' Steven said crisply.

"You think Miss McAllister will mind my coming?'' Max was suddenly nervous.

"Not at all. She's a wonderful woman, Gilly. What makes Bronte happy makes Gilly happy. Bronte was very upset when she heard you weren't allowed to come.''

"Well I'm here,'' said Max, lifting his thin shoulders and grinning triumphantly to himself. "If the worst comes to the worst and someone comes for me I'll make a bolt for the rain forest. Live wild. Anyone could take refuge in there without being found.''

"It mightn't come to that,'' Steven told him in a dry, matter-of-fact voice. "Your father might be persuaded to see reason.''

"I wouldn't like to be hanging by my thumbs waiting for that,'' Max groaned.

"You've got to believe in yourself, Max.'' Steven glanced at the boy, the quality of his tone sympathetic but somehow adamant.

"A guy like you would be born believing in himself,'' Max said, experiencing the strange sensation Steven, who oozed self confidence without a shred of the arrogance Max was sick to death of, was holding out a helping hand.

"Not always, Max,'' Steven declared. "At your age I was just as much in need of guidance and encouragement. Hang in there. Try not to get too upset. Bronte told me you're a straight A student. That means you've got a head start on being anything you want.''

"So long as I don't turn out like my father,'' said Max. Slumped back in the seat he suddenly straightened, his face

lighting up like a light had been switched on inside him.
''We're home! Gee, that's great! I can't wait to see Bronte.
I've missed her so much.''

Bronte retreated to the bow window to get a breeze. She
couldn't really concentrate on what she was doing because
Steven Randolph was forever on her mind. In fact it was
getting so bad she often went off into long spells just thinking
about him, coming back to reality with a start. She'd been in
such a state when he brought her home from Christine's party
it took her days to recover. Despite all the pep talks she had
got into the habit of giving herself, she had done the unthink-
able. She had fallen head over heels in love with a man she
didn't really know.

It was shocking when you thought about it. Only a short
time ago she'd been on the verge of marrying Nathan
Saunders. At one time she had even convinced herself she
was as much in love with Nat as she was ever going to be
with any man. Although life with her mother's ghastly mega-
rich husband had been enough to put her right off men. She'd
then seen Gilly's splendid isolation as an alternate lifestyle
but Steven Randolph had cured her of that. He'd torn down
all the defences she'd built up. He'd brought her to full life.
Even with only a foretaste he'd shown her what making love
was all about. Kisses alone were enough to make her surrender. Yet it wasn't simply sexual attraction, overwhelming as
it got, sometimes she thought he had the trick of seeing
through to her soul.

Steven touched her deeply on so many levels. She *liked*
him. She liked everything about him. The way he shared
jokes with Gilly. The way his eyes lit up with real affection
for her great-aunt. She'd escaped up here to Gilly wanting
nothing more than peace and quiet. Instead she met Steven.
A life changing guy. A guy every girl dreamed about. A guy
who had an older woman called Christine very much in love
with him. Did Steven realize it? That was the question.

Bronte had the dismal notion Christine might put up a fierce fight for him, perhaps in unseen ways.

As she sat there brooding, forgetting the time, she saw Steven's 4WD emerge from the tunnel of poincianas now in glorious bloom. It rounded the circular drive that enclosed the fountain, coming to a halt at the base of the steps. She could see plainly someone sitting beside him in the passenger seat.

Oh my goodness! Bronte flew up from the window seat erupting into cries of joy. "Gilly, Gilly, come quickly. It's Steven and he's got Max with him. I can't believe it. I mean I *can't* believe it!" She was literally dancing with joy.

"Darling, darling, Max!" Bronte hurled herself at her half brother, using the front steps at a launching pad. "You're here. It's like a miracle you were allowed to come."

Steven watched the two embrace. It was so emotional he almost had to turn away. Here were two young people who had suffered such emotional deprivation in childhood and adolescence much as he had suffered himself, although Bronte, at least, had had one wonderful woman in her life, Gilly.

Gilly now appeared on the verandah, wiping her hands on the floral apron tied around her waist. "Well, well, well," she cried. "Come up here, young fella and say hello." Gilly's snapping black eyes moved on to Steven. "Hi, there, Steven. How did you get to deliver our boy?"

"He found me literally falling by the wayside." Max flung Steven a grateful glance, his arm flung around Bronte's shoulder. "I'm not used to this sun. Boy is it *hot!* And I wasn't wearing a hat. It seemed like a miracle when Steven drove up."

"I think we'll get Max out of the sun, Bronte, and give him a cool drink," Steven said with a smile.

"Come on up, boy," Gilly called cheerfully. "*I* think it's a bloody miracle you're here."

It wasn't until a full ten minutes later when they were

sitting in the cool of the fern filled Garden Room that Steven gave Max a tiny prod. At the same time he nodded encouragingly at the boy. Max up to this point had allowed Bronte and Gilly to believe he had been given permission to spend the vacation with them.

Gilly's sharp eyes caught the movement but Bronte sitting between Max and Steven was so charged with pleasure and excitement she missed it.

"Something to tell us, Max?" Gilly prompted. He was achingly like Bronte even to the beautiful eloquent blue-violet eyes. Miranda's eyes, of course. But he appeared worryingly on the frail side, adolescent arms like sticks. His legs beneath those hot trousers would be the same.

Max took another gulp of his cold drink then put his head in his hands.

"You've run away, haven't you?" Bronte suddenly divined, putting her hand on his back and rubbing it. "I knew it was too good to be true!"

"Don't get jittery, Bronte," Max begged, lifting his dark head.

"That's right," Steven seconded, sounding firm. "Max's father might be persuaded to allow Max to stay."

"And maybe he'll buy me a guitar. I've always wanted one. And a Ferrari when I get my licence. Sorry, Steven, you don't know my father. He's heartless."

"Maybe I know someone who *does* know him." Steven said.

That took Bronte's breath away. She turned to stare into Steven's striking face, never forgetting what this man could do—already had done—to her. "Who are you, Steven? You have friends everywhere."

"That's far from unusual." He smiled into her troubled eyes. "Max left his mother a note, so she knows where he was heading."

"Maybe we could pretend I never got here," Max suggested, looking from one to the other. "It's not as though I'd be a huge loss."

"That was brave running away, Max," Bronte said, studying her young half brother with deep concern. "Carl is used to total capitulation. He'll insist you go back."

"I don't think I'd survive it if he did another job on me," Max confessed, looking all of a sudden deeply depressed.

Steven's face tautened into a dark golden mask. "What are we talking about here, physical abuse?"

Max coloured violently, but managed a strangled laugh. "Why do you think my mother shoved me into boarding school as soon as they'd take me. Because my dear old dad likes to hit into me. I wasn't his kind of kid. I'm a geek. As I got older he took to me with his fists. I couldn't count the number of times Bronte got between me and him."

"God in Heaven!" said Gilly, turning ashen. "You're not going to tell me he's struck you, Bronte?" She looked with horror across the glass topped table at her great-niece.

"Boarding school was my refuge, too," Bronte said, in a low voice. "He never touched me unless I got in the way. Max has always been his victim."

Gilly took off her glasses and scrubbed her eyes hard. "How absolutely appalling. Something must be done. What sort of a mother is Miranda?" she asked, helplessly.

"I would imagine she's terrified of him, too," Steven said, trying to bank down the anger these disclosures were generating in him.

"He doesn't hit *her*," Max said.

"Not that you can *see*." Steven's smooth voice rasped. "I can't tell you who this person is I know, but I can ask them to have a word with your father, Max."

Immediately Max looked to Steven as a hero. "Do you think it would work? What could he say? He must be a powerful person like my father?"

"It's someone who knows a great deal about Carl Brandt."

"And how did you meet him exactly?" Bronte wanted to know. So much mystery surrounded Steven. So much he wouldn't say, yet he seemed to know the most important people in the country.

He narrowed his green eyes at her. "I didn't exactly say if it was a him or a her. Trust me, Bronte. That's all I ask."

"I'm ready to trust you," Max declared. "There's nothing I want more than to be able to stay."

"Well I'll see what I can do," Steven promised. "We'll have to work fast. Days have elapsed."

"He's probably already sent someone after me," Max said, a wealth of sorrow in his voice.

"Bank on it," Bronte muttered.

"I'm sorry if I've got you worried," Max grabbed Bronte's hand. "I thought I was being my own man for a change, but I've probably made a huge mistake."

"Let me try to deal with it," Steven suggested briskly. "I'll need to make a couple of calls which I'll do now." He stood up. "After that, if you're up to it, Max, after all your travels, you might like to join Bronte and me. I'm taking her out to Wildwood. It's a wild life park."

"Crocs?" Max asked, his eyes lighting up.

"Twenty-footers," Steven said with a smile.

Max made a jump-back in his chair. "Lead the way. I vowed I was going to have a good time for once."

Bronte examined the school clothes he had on. "You can't go in that. You'll be too hot."

"All I've got is some underwear and my pyjamas," Max announced. "Can't I go then?"

Gilly guffawed. "Course you can go. Bronte didn't mean that. You can rustle up something for him to wear, Bronte. Unisex stuff. A plain T-shirt and a pair of khaki shorts. He's pretty skinny. We'll have to fatten him up. If Steven can work his usual miracles and Max stays, we'll have to take him into town and buy him some gear. I've got an akubra that will fit you, son, and some sandals. Home made sunscreen to protect you as well.''

"No wonder Bronte loves you, Gilly," Max said, going around the table to give her a spontaneous kiss.

They arrived at feeding time at the crocodile farm, joining a crowd of tourists to watch behind the fenced enclosure as Charles "Chika" Moran, Steven's partner, threw the biggest and most dangerous crocodile fondly known by the staff as King Tut its rations for the day. There were mingled cries of excitement and revulsion as the great horny monster, slate grey in colour with a buttery yellow belly and fangs as long and thick as a man's finger, took the big chunks of meat— it looked like pork?—with deadly efficiency. The enormous pink cave of its throat opened wide, jaws snapped audibly on flesh and bone. Nothing went to waste.

Ugh!

Bronte glanced at Max's face under the dusty brown akubra. It was bright with heat, interest and excitement in equal measure. Beads of perspiration stood out on his nose, above his lip and around his temples. His eyes were glittering.

"I wouldn't do that for anything!" He turned his head briefly to give them a big grin. "Aren't they brutes! That guy, Chika, must be sick of living. Did you see how fast it came out of the pool at him. I'd drop dead with fright. And the way it bolted the food. How much can a croc eat in one day? It disappeared down its throat in a second."

"A full grown croc can swallow a man in one piece," Steven informed him. "That fellow and the others you're going to see are saltwater crocs, the most feared of all crocodiles. The fresh water croc grows to less than half that fellow's size. King Tut is a good six metres, maybe a bit more. Saltwater, estuarine crocodiles, attack and kill human beings as we know. In the wild, they'll attack anything man or beast that invades their territory. The freshwater croc of the north is harmless to man. It only eats fish. Even so I wouldn't get in the water with them. They look much the same as the salties except they're much smaller and the snout is narrower and more pointed.''

''They're classed as reptiles, aren't they?'' Max asked.

Steven nodded. ''Part of the order of reptiles that includes alligators, caymans and gavials. Australia is home to a great variety of reptiles. Venomous and non-venomous land snakes, a fantastic number of lizards that look fearsome but are quite harmless although the Outback goanna can do a bit of damage. We've yet to come to the python pit. The Queensland scrub python is just about the same length as that croc, twenty plus feet.''

''Cool!'' Max said happily.

The fathomless dome of the sky was cloudless and of a blue that drenched the senses. Water birds wheeled overhead shrieking and honking. Parakeets and lorikeets exploded from the trees in flashing waves of brilliant colour—emerald, red, royal blue, yellow and purple. Lagoons adorned the park, ponds the water birds called home. Deeper into the park lay the breeding lakes where thousands of crocodiles, an incredible sight, lazed around the banks.

As they entered the park that afternoon a great flock of cockatoos fluttered like white flowers amid the greenery, while on the ground stately peacocks paraded slowly and majestically across the thick carpet of grass. The males offered a gorgeous visual treat spreading their brilliantly marked feathers with their spotted ''eyes'' into a metallic greenish train with deep violet-blue underparts.

''Fancy the Romans roasting and eating such glorious birds,'' Bronte remarked.

''Fancy the female, the peahen, being so drab,'' Steven smiled. ''It just doesn't seem right.''

''Proud as a peacock. That's *male*,'' Bronte returned sweetly.

Later they got to meet Steven's partner, Chika, a very affable "character" dressed all in khaki, slouch hat, khaki shirt, shorts, with the Wildwood logo of a grinning crocodile adorned by a gold crown, on the breast pocket of the shirt. He told them with the greatest satisfaction business was booming.

"Best thing I ever did was take on Steven for a partner." Chika clapped a massive sun speckled, largely fingerless, hand on Steven's shoulder, his expression quite fatherly." I know my end of the business but young as he is, Steven leaves me for dead. Course he's a trained lawyer which helps when it comes to knowing your way around all the rules and regulations, accounting, that sort of thing. He's turned the park into a regular show place as you can see. Cleaned it right up. The tourists love it."

"It's a great mystery how our aborigines consistently managed to survive the hazards of life in the tropical wilds," Bronte said.

"The crocs are their brothers, that's why," Chika explained. "Their totem protects them. That's the reason they cross the croc infested waters of the Gulf like nothing is gonna to happen. And it doesn't. The same goes for sharks. They believe in their totem. Spirit protection. It works for them but not for us blokes. I've had my near-misses as you might notice. You, young fella—" He turned to Max with a friendly smile. "What are yah doin' up here with that shining pink face? Yah'll have to get yourself a tan."

"If I stay!" Max breathed.

"What's he mean?" Chika met his partner's eyes.

"Long story, Chika, but he wants to stay."

"Want to come with me while I continue my rounds?" Chika asked the boy. "Lot of things you mightn't notice unless I point them out. Sometimes even I can't make out what's right under me nose. Wild animals have a way of camouflaging themselves."

"Love to," said Max jauntily.

"Don't let him near the cassowary," Bronte called as they

moved off. She referred to the massive, long legged flightless bird that lived in the rain forests of northern Australia and New Guinea. Cassowaries were very cantankerous birds.

"For some reason they hate cars with a metallic dark blue or dark grey paint," Steven said. "They like to attack them."

"Perhaps they see their own reflections in the glossy surface and fancy it's another bird?" Bronte suggested.

"That's a theory." Steven smiled. There was an intense pleasure just looking at her. She was wearing a white, lace trimmed top with a very pretty floral skirt that flared out as she walked. The skin on her bare slender legs had gained a gold lustre. He could stare at her all day. Instead he continued speaking in a conversational tone. "Cassowaries are capable of leaping over two metres, so I've had the fences around the enclosures raised. Their claws are effective weapons as you know. Mercifully only the odd bird seems to want to vault the fences, but all wild animals are highly unpredictable. That includes our cuddly little koalas. Feel like an icecream? We can sit by the lake and watch the swans."

"That would be lovely." Bronte gave a pleasurable sigh. Just the way he was looking at her caused little ripples to fan right through her body. What a wonder there was in being in love! What heartbreak if he wasn't actually in love with her. She had to face the fact it might only be chemistry on his side.

While Steven moved off to the kiosk, Bronte wandered down to the edge of the ornamental lake. It was partially covered by the beautiful blue lotus lily, the perimeters of the pond fringed with water reeds, iris and thick stands of the boat shaped Spoon Lilies loading the air with their delicious perfume. The native black swans, their scarlet bills banded with white, sailed gracefully across the green glassy surface. Such a lovely peaceful scene, but she had too much on her mind to fully appreciate it.

Timber picnic tables with attached bench seats were set beneath the great shade trees in the area. A family with several mildly squabbling children in tow sat a distance off. Bronte chose one of the empty tables, delicately lifting one leg then the other to sit on the timber bench. She'd been wearing a rather elegant new wide-brimmed straw hat she'd bought along with many other purchases in the town, now she took it off her head and placed it on the table. Her step-father knew where Max was. He knew how to find him.

She stared sightlessly at the glittering water, the stately progress of the swans. No sense any of them trying to fool themselves. Max was in deep trouble. The harsh reality was no one crossed Carl Brandt, certainly not his fifteen-year-old son. She could just imagine her stepfather's anger and incre-dulity reverberating around the house. That thundering voice!

"He *what?* He dared to do *what?*"

She could hear her mother's half baked entreaties—making sure she stood well back from this spine-chilling man she had married.

"I'll show him. The disobedient little bastard. How could he possibly think I'd *stand* for this? I'll set the police on him. And that little bitch of a Bronte, after all I've done for her! Running up to North Queensland to a crazy old woman. Your kids, Miranda, are drop-outs." The last with a rising ear-splitting bellow.

The miracle was those drop-out kids didn't use drugs with the parents fate had dealt them.

Facing the lake Bronte didn't see Steven until he lightly touched her shoulder. "Mango ice-cream coming up. You'd better eat it fast."

"Thank you." Bronte took the cone in her hand and set her tongue to work. It was absolutely delicious.

"You were looking very serious when I came up," Steven observed after a few minutes of enjoying their ice creams. His eyes met hers.

"Was I?" She finished the crisp cone, accepting the paper napkin Steven passed her to wipe her fingers. "I was imag-ining my stepfather's wrath. He'd never expect Max to flout his wishes, to get on a bus and a train and travel up to us. He'll be furious. He's quite mad. He'll pick up the phone and call the police.''

''I don't think so,'' Steven said with quiet self-possession. ''You've heard nothing so far.''

''Well, then he'll send one of his goons,'' she told him. ''I know it's a dreadful thing to say but I hope and hope one of these days my stepfather will stop breathing. He's been trying to break Max since he was a child. I've been thinking about what you said about my mother.''

''That Brandt might beat her, too?'' He encircled her wrist with his fingertips. A light touch. Extraordinarily intimate.

''I'd take to him with scissors if he did,'' Bronte said, feeling she couldn't handle such a thing. ''I've never *seen* him touch her, and she has never said a word. But underneath all the show, I believe she's just as frightened of him as we were. Too frightened to get away. And then there's this business of your knowing someone, Steven. Can't you tell me who it is?'' She kept her eyes on him, seeing her own reflection.

''I'll tell you, Bronte, when I get my answer,'' Steven told her. ''I'd like you to trust me until then.''

''All right.'' She inclined her head in acquiescence. ''When I woke up this morning I felt the strangest thing,'' she confessed. ''I felt your lips on mine.''

Such a disclosure lifted the sexual excitement between them. He pulled her closer to him. ''The night of the party when I finally got to bed your perfume was all over me. I'd taken you in through my pores. I've never wanted a woman in my life like I want you Bronte. I want to take you home with me right now. Would you come? Look up.'' She had bent her dark lustrous head against the ardour of his gaze. ''Look at me. Answer my question.''

The thing mounting between them had her obeying his will. ''There are things about you, Steven, that trouble me.''

She ought to say it. "Who are you *really?* What part does Christine play in your life? You're obviously very...*close.*"

He gave a brief laugh, not smooth, slightly harsh. "I thought I told you, Bronte. Christine is my friend, my business partner, not my lover."

"Men lie," she said sombrely, provoking him a little. "Have you at any time thought you could fall in love with her?"

He looked straight over her head for a moment. "I find her a delight to look at. I'm susceptible to a woman's beauty, and she's an excellent, trustworthy business partner. I can't begin to answer that question, Bronte. Christine has been a woman mourning her dead husband. She's quite a bit older than I am. Did you know?"

"Is it important?" She felt a stab of pain she recognised as jealousy. It shamed her.

"Not anymore." His gaze came back to rest on her face. "I've wanted no one but you from the moment I laid eyes on you."

"Because you imagine I'd be wonderful to make love to?" she challenged. Her looks, her perceived desirability weren't all there was to her. "I could be a big disappointment."

"Do the stars come out at night?" he asked, in a gentle mocking voice. "You don't have to prove anything to me, Bronte. You only have to be yourself. We both know there would be no disappointments. Can't you see you're physically perfect to me?"

She pulled back and looked at him. "So what is it about my character you want to change?"

"Not much." He lifted a hand, let it slip to the back of her neck causing all those little ripples to start up again. "I know we can get rid of the prickles in time."

"I mightn't feel myself without them. So who's going to be first to meet the parents?" she asked." You seem to know mine. I know you lost your mother. I *know* you loved her deeply. I know there's big trauma somewhere there. I don't know your father, or your brother who I take it is your father's heir. You've now met Max though I'm not sure for how long he will be here. Maybe my whole wretched life caused me to fall into your arms. Maybe as an excellent businessman—no doubt it's genetic—you see me as an asset. Like Nat did.''

His hand moved. "You escaped Saunders," he said crisply. "Probably the best thing you've ever done."

"Don't be angry with me." She realized what she'd said had upset and disturbed him.

"I'm trying not to be."

"I need time, Steven," she said. "Do you mind? I've made one huge mistake in my life."

"You think what's happening between us is going too fast?"

"Isn't it? You've come into my life like a *force*. There's a good chance both of us could be swept away. I can't follow you just like that! What we have might be thrilling, but I don't yet know what it means. You have this project going with Gilly. Is it going to work out as well as you both think? I have a young brother who's about to feel the severity of his father's outrage. Carl has no control over me anymore, but he's not about to leave Max do as he likes. Max toes the line. I expect when Max is taken back, he'll get it with both fists.''

Steven's clear green eyes darkened. "Wild animals behave better than that. Your stepfather is a dangerous man. He should be stopped. Not only for Max's sake, but for your mother's. I don't know if you can see it, but the same thing anchors us, Bronte. We both hate men like Carl Brandt. Destructive men. I expect he's spent much of his life trying to cover his tracks, thinking he's succeeded, inspiring fear But you know, there's always *somebody,* somewhere, who holds the key to their downfall. No wrong-doer can ever really feel safe."

"No one has been able to touch him so far," Bronte stated,

obeying the powerful impulse to lean, if only for a moment, against his shoulder.

His hand slipped down her spine to her waist. He bent his face to her flushed cheek, inhaling her fragrance. "There's always the element of chance, Bronte." His voice promised hope. "Chance saves lives. Destroys them, too. A man takes an earlier plane. It crashes into a mountain. Another man misses the plane by a few minutes. His life is saved. Supposing you hadn't met me? Supposing I hadn't met you. Supposing Max hadn't found the guts to flee, to admit to the physical abuse he's suffered at the hands of his father. It's all happened. The wheels have been set in motion."

"Do you know how good that sounds?" She lifted her head to stare into his eyes. There was such strength of purpose in him. But what of her and Max? Her darling Gilly at a time of life when she shouldn't have to endure a bad experience. "Surely there are risks involved?"

His lips moved across her hair. "There are always risks associated with freedom. You're ready for them, aren't you?"

"I'm ready for anything as long as you're near me." It wasn't something she meant to say, but she did, even though it was *so* revealing.

"I will be," he said. "Do you know how good it is sitting here with you, half in half out of my arms?"

She relaxed pressing her body closer to him, deriving much comfort from contact with his body.

"You know how to touch me, don't you? Not just my body, my heart."

"Why is that so strange?" he asked, the erotic current between them strongly humming. "I love your eyes, the way they mirror your every passing emotion. The ineffable colour. I love your hair. I love your lustrous skin. I love your throat. I especially love your mouth. Do you suppose anyone would notice if I kissed you?"

She took a quick look over his shoulder. "There are at

least twenty people looking this way already,'' she told him shakily. She couldn't stop him once his lips touched hers.

"You can shut your eyes, okay?"

"Steven—" Her heart leapt. There was no such thing as a casual kiss from *him.* Kisses like Steven's should be greeted with rapturous applause.

"All right," he relented. "I'll catch up later. You can be sure of that. In any case, here comes brother Max. He's a nice kid who's shown the guts to really make something of himself. He looks like he's been enjoying himself with Chika.''

Bronte smiled, feeling her veins flowing with love and affection. She swung her head following the direction of Steven's gaze. Max was loping along the gravelled path with gangly grace. He saw them and waved. He looked like he didn't have a care in the world. The sight wrung her heart. "The last thing I'm going to do is hand him over to his father," Bronte vowed, her voice breaking a little with emotion. "I'm so proud of him. I underestimated his grit."

Steven's handsome face assumed a resolute expression. "It's all about fighting the fear, isn't it? You had to fight the fear to call off your wedding. That took courage. Severity breeds fear. Fear breeds hate. Max has made his first step towards freedom. We have to help him."

So in this way it was settled. They all banded together to oppose a tyrant called Carl Brandt.

CHAPTER EIGHT

IT WAS midmorning. Gilly and Max who were getting on like a house on fire had gone on a discovery trek in the rain forest. Bronte was still at her self-imposed job of cataloguing the contents of the very large homestead. New things were always turning up, not surprising in a family of collectors going back generations. The General's collection alone could fill a warehouse.

She went to the bow window as she heard a vehicle coming up the drive. It couldn't be Steven. He had appointments in town. Who else? All of them were haunted by fears maybe the police would arrive, or one of Carl Brandt's strong men looking for Max. They were fears neither Max nor Bronte could shake off. Gilly, on the other hand, living in isolation told them she had a gun licence. Whether that was true or not Bronte didn't know. All she knew was Gilly in her younger days had been a crack shot. For that matter Gilly had taught her how to handle a rifle and look after one.

Now the vehicle, a big 4WD with a bull bar entered the circular drive.

"Oh no!" She reeled back, half stunned, her skin tingling with shock. It was her stepfather himself! It couldn't be. He let other people do his dirty work. Where was her mother? At least her mother tried to put the brakes on his violent outbursts. There was someone sitting in the passenger seat. In another moment she would know who it was.

It didn't seem possible. She felt sick to the pit of her stomach. It was Nat Saunders. What had Nat Saunders to do with anything? Anger fuelled her. She and Nat were finished. Over!

She made a mad rush to the nearest phone, punching in

Steven's mobile number which she had memorized. Memorizing numbers was something that came easily to her. Now she thanked God for it. It had saved precious time.

It took an eternity for Steven to answer. She peered down the hallway. They were out of the vehicle walking towards the steps. Invasion. She could feel every nerve in her body jumping.

When she heard Steven's voice, the relief was enormous. "Steven, listen," she spoke rapidly, her voice a near whisper. "He's here. He's come." They were at the front door. She jumped at the sight of them. "Brandt." She put a name to her visitor and hurriedly replaced the receiver.

Bronte took a deep shuddering breath and squared her shoulders, reminding herself how far she had come. "What are you doing here?" she demanded, in a hard, tight voice, walking to the open door.

Brandt barely looked at her. Without answering, her step-father pushed her out of the way and stalked into the house, staring first into the drawing room, then the formal dining room where she'd been working. "Where's Max?" he rasped, jabbing a finger at her.

"He's not here." She steeled herself for what came next. A slap to take her head off? This was a man who knew nothing about anger management. Frustration turned to violence at terrifying speed.

"I said, where *is* he?"

"Do you think I'd tell you when you're in this mood." She had to be crazy getting in his way.

"As soon as I find him—"

"You're going to do what?" Bronte burst out contemptuously. "Beat the hell out of him?"

Nat Saunders, caught between admiration and anxiety, spoke for the first time. "Bronte, please stop. Tell your step-father where Max is. That's your duty. Carl has a right to know. He's his father."

"Some father!" Bronte said with disgust. "He's been terrorizing Max for most of his life. You approve of that, do you, Nat, you gutless wimp!'' Her heart pounded violently against her ribs as Carl Brandt's face changed. It was so cold, she feared he would attack her.

''Bronte, be reasonable.'' Moving clumsily, Nat got between Bronte and her stepfather. ''You weren't part of this. You're the innocent bystander. Max planned it all. There's no point in trying to protect him.''

''Isn't there?'' Bronte forced herself to stay put. ''What's your position on child abuse, Nat?''

Nat eyed her uncertainly. Bronte, he knew, was a firecracker. ''I certainly don't condone it. All Carl wants is his son and Max deserves some punishment for putting his parents through the wringer.''

''What makes you think they're *normal?*'' Bronte challenged. ''Where's my mother,'' she demanded to know, willing Gilly and Max to stay away. Entering the house from the rear garden as they would, they wouldn't see the 4WD parked in the drive.

''Forget your mother!'' Brandt suddenly picked up a valuable Chinese vase and hurled it against the wall. ''Don't waste another minute on her,'' he barked. Then to Nat Saunders, the direct order. ''Search the house. The little bastard is cowering somewhere. Probably in a closet.''

For a moment Nat couldn't seem to move. He stood staring at the shattered vase on the parquet floor as though contemplating the best way to mend it. ''Maybe we should wait it out, Carl,'' he suggested. ''At least until we speak to Miss McAllister. She does own the place. And that vase.''

''Dammit!'' Brandt exploded in extreme irritation, a big man, heavy shouldered, an angry flush on his face. ''You'll never get Bronte back if you keep acting like a bloody girl.''

''Get me *back!*'' Bronte gave her ex-fiancé an angry, alarmed glance. ''For goodness' sake, there's no way in the world you'll ever get me back, Nathan. I'm the one who jilted you, remember? Have you gone crazy? What are you doing teaming up with this violent man?''

"I wanted to see you, Bronte," Nat said, staring at her with intensity. "I love you. I can't stop loving you. Dammit, you must still love me?''

"I don't love you, Nat. If I'd loved you I would have married you. I'm sorry. End of story."

"The two of you shut up before I throw up," Carl Brandt bellowed. "You better do exactly what I say, Saunders. Search the house. You don't think I'm going to let my own kid make a fool out of me."

"All he was asking was to come for a holiday," Bronte cried, pressure building up in her. "He needs a holiday. Why couldn't you let him have it? Why are you such a monster?''

Brandt barked a laugh. "It's a pity poor little Maxie isn't more like you. He might have had a chance." He strode away looking like he was capable of tearing the whole house apart.

Nat lingered bravely. "Bronte, tell him what he wants to know. Only a fool crosses Carl Brandt, even my dad says so, and for a very good reason. He's a dangerous man."

Bronte bit her lip until she tasted blood. "All the more reason why I'm not going to hand Max over to him."

"I feel half scared to death myself," Nat admitted. "I've only done this for you. I don't care all that much what happens to Max. Maybe he'll get a cuff around the ears. Where is he? You saw how Brandt smashed that vase. It looks valuable. I would think close to three or four thousand. Best not to push him. He's perfectly capable of smashing the entire house."

"Well then, I'd better ring the police."

"Won't they ask why you're keeping Max from his own father? The boy disobeyed him. Your mother seemed frantic when I last saw her."

"Which was when?" Bronte asked with deep concern.

"Before we left, I saw her at the house. She had a lot of make-up on but I spotted the black eye."

Bronte winced. "How did it happen?"

"How should I know? You can bet your life she didn't walk into a door."

"He's got to be stopped," Bronte said.

"How? He's like an express train barging into a station."

"I'm not giving up Max," Bronte said with great fervour.

"Bronte, I can't protect you." Nat put his two hands to his head in anguish. "I want to but Carl could tear me apart. Sometimes I think he's completely mad."

To confirm it, a bellow like Krakatoa erupting made Nat's whole body twitch and shudder. "I have to go help him, Bronte," he said apologetically, fear warring with his need to stay with her. "Tell me where the kid is hiding? I'll try to get him back home in one piece."

Fifteen minutes elapsed during which the two men searched the house, the raised area beneath the house where only a possum could fit and the home grounds. If Gilly and Max were anywhere near the rain forest fringe they would glimpse them going about their search. Bronte consoled herself with the thought. No one could find Gilly in there if she chose to hide. Gilly would have made any Guerrilla Brigade. That was Bronte's only consolation. But they couldn't hide forever.

Bronte headed towards the cupboard where she knew Gilly had hidden the .22. She'd really need a .303 to stop a charging rhino like Brandt. This was all bad, she thought. She didn't want anything to do with guns. Guns did terrible damage. On the other hand in dire straits they were protection. Her stepfather wasn't such a fool he wouldn't take her seriously if she had a rifle in hand. With a surge of triumph she realized Brandt knew she wasn't frightened of him anymore. Or, at least, not frightened enough to turn to jelly.

Nevertheless she was trembling all over as she approached the cupboard, hearing her stepfather roaring instructions at Nat. A cold sick sweat broke out on her. The rifle wasn't there. Of course. Gilly had shifted it. Where was Steven?

Please, please, Steven, where are you? Even if he'd left his meeting straight away it would take him ages to drive to the plantation.

Moments later Bronte was faced by Nat looking like he was suffering from heat exhaustion and her stepfather's raging anger. Brandt's bared teeth and his blazing eyes, the high flush on his skin, made him look more like a devil than a man. "This is the last time I'm going to ask you, you stupid little cow. *Where's my son!*"

Bronte surprised herself by bellowing back. "Out there somewhere. Gone into hiding. In case you haven't noticed, we have a jungle on our doorstep."

"You're lying!" Brandt suddenly grabbed her by the shoulders and shook her like a doll.

"Carl. Stop it. Leave her alone." Nat summoned all his courage.

For answer, Brandt hurled Bronte across the entrance hall with such force she bounced off the wall, tumbling against a console where she cracked her head. For long moments she saw stars.

"That's disgusting." Nat, inches shorter, stones lighter, leapt at the older man, beginning to struggle with him, before he, too, went flying. "Don't move the both of you," Brandt snarled through clenched teeth. "I can wait this out. They've got to come in sometime."

Bronte straightened up, dazed from the whack to the back of her head. She put a hand to it. There was quite a lump. A few feet from her Nat sat huddled up, numb with shock.

Nothing in his pampered, privileged life had prepared Nat Saunders for a man like Carl Brandt. The rage of the man, the power! The mad glare. He'd thought he'd known his father's sometime partner now he realized all these years of respecting Brandt's Midas touch, he didn't know him at all. Now the very sight of the man repulsed him. The thought of what might happen to Bronte, to Max, even himself, terrified Nat. In his world people were civilised, not violent.

Casting a subduing glance at them as though they were a pair of impertinent children, Brandt walked quickly to the front verandah as the sound of a helicopter's whirling rotors split the air.

"Who the hell's this?" he yelled back at Bronte.

Instantly Bronte forgot her sore head. "The police," she taunted. "I was ringing them when you arrived."

"Thank goodness!" Nat moaned, quite taken in. "They ought to put men like your stepfather in a maximum security prison."

"It's not a police helicopter," Brandt contradicted her, his voice flat and cold. "Whoever it is, get rid of them fast. Hear me?" He strode back into the entrance hall, standing intimidatingly over Bronte. While Nat stared up at him in wordless awe and disgust, Bronte rose shakily to her feet, unable to conceal the tremendous relief she was feeling. She knew in her bones it was Steven. The way she'd sounded on the phone, he obviously had gone to great lengths to get here. Even to commandeering a chopper. "This is most probably a friend of mine," she announced, visibly sparking up. "What are you going to do? Fight us all?"

Fury and an answering triumph flashed in Brandt's eyes. "If you want to save your little half brother from the hiding he deserves, you'll get rid of your friend quickly and quietly," he advised.

Bronte ran past him, down the steps, hurling herself into Steven's waiting arms. "Oh thank goodness, you're here," she cried, revelling in the strength of his grasp. "Gilly and Max are somewhere in the forest. They would have seen them searching the grounds and decided not to come in."

"Them?" he queried sharply. "How many?"

"I never in my wildest dreams—"

What Bronte was going to say next was interrupted by Brandt's voice, booming from the verandah as though he'd levelled a megaphone at them. "You'll have to speak to your friend there, Bronte," he ordered. "You can't come inside."

Steven continued walking drawing Bronte with him. "Why, if it isn't the universally loathed Carl Brandt. It's been a long time."

Brandt's head went up like a wild animal's sensing the approach of a man with a gun. He appeared to recognise Steven's voice. Now they were close enough for him to see Steven's face.

"Many years," Brandt grated, causing Bronte to stare at Steven in consternation. They knew each other and she had no idea? "Unpleasant as it is to renew your acquaintance, may I ask what you're doing here?"

"I thought it would give us an opportunity to talk." Steven dropped his arm from Bronte's shoulders, mounting the steps. Tall, powerful, lean, confronting the older man, heavy of build, but not a vestige of fat on him.

"Talk?" Brandt was breathing hard through his nostrils like a bull about to charge. "All I'm here for is my boy. My son." Even so he spoke in a remarkably restrained voice for him. "This has nothing to do with you."

"It has a lot to do with me," Steven contradicted. "Bronte and her great-aunt Gillian are my friends. I've met Max. I like him. I've been hearing how you've treated him over the years. Most probably Bronte's mother as well. You like hurting people, don't you, Brandt? I'd say you were a sadist."

Brandt laughed as if at a joke. "I'm not getting into any conversation with you, Saunders. Your slug of a cousin is cowering somewhere inside."

"Saunders?" Bronte felt shell-shocked. "What's he talking about?" She turned wild eyes on Steven.

"Don't you *know*, Bronte?" Her stepfather worked hard on a chuckle. "I heard he was calling himself by his mother's maiden name. Randolph. Fine, conservative people, the Randolphs. The kind that would never allow the likes of me into their home." He raised his voice to the familiar bellow that would have shattered a glass. "Come out and meet your cousin, Nathan," he invited with fierce enjoyment. "Believe it or not, he appears to have stolen your girl.'' He laughed again as if at a good joke.

"Oh!'' Nat stood moaning at the door. ''It really is *you,* Steven.''

A shiver passed through Bronte's body and brain. She'd thought herself pretty smart. Now she had to seriously reconsider her position.

"Long time no see, Nat,'' Steven responded. ''What do you think you're up to coming here with the likes of Brandt? I knew you did stupid things I just didn't realize how often.''

"And you're so clever,'' Nat flushed hotly. ''If you must know I came all the way up here to ask Bronte to come back to me.''

Steven's laugh held no humour. ''Then you can waddle all the way back. Just how much does it take to get through to you? Bronte wants no part of you.''

Nat looked genuinely unconvinced. ''Let her speak for herself, you arrogant so and so.''

Steven turned his mahogany head towards the speechless Bronte. ''So what do you want to tell him, Bronte?''

Bronte's voice went brittle with anger. ''What other shocks are there in store for me, I wonder?'' Her violet eyes flashed. ''Steven Randolph aka Steven Saunders who just happens to be my ex-fiancé's cousin.''

"Steven turned his back on his family years ago,'' Nat said, making it sound the worst of the seven deadly sins. ''His mother died of cancer but he blamed his father for it. My uncle Bryce is a wonderful man but Steven wouldn't have that. He was too much his mother's son. There are dark places in good old Steven. He despises the rest of us. That's why he changed his name by deed poll to Randolph. My uncle Bryce heads up the big legal firm—Radcliffe-Reed. Surely you know that? Surely you remember meeting my cousin, Lyall, Steven's older brother, at our engagement party?''

Bronte groaned at the pain in her head. ''To tell you the

truth I do. I didn't like him. Pompous. Self-satisfied. Talked to everyone like they were half witted. Maybe it's all the legal training. He didn't look in the least like Steven. He looked more like you.''

Why oh why hadn't Steven told her all this, Bronte thought furiously. But she wasn't going to start a fight with him in front of her sneering stepfather, or the self-righteous Nat.

''Could you talk about this another time?'' Brandt barked with hateful sarcasm.

''What's there to talk about?'' Steven snapped, looking like a man who had to be treated with great caution.

''We've got to move on from here,'' Brandt told him angrily. ''If you want my stepdaughter and you look like you do, you're welcome to her. She's a real little shrew who keeps getting in the way. I want my son. It will be good to see him again. I intend to take him home to his mother.''

''Who has a beautiful black eye,'' Nat volunteered. Brandt didn't look half so dangerous stacked up beside his cousin Steven, he decided. Steven looked amazingly fit. Older, tougher, a lot more formidable than he remembered.

''She took it into her head to oppose me,'' Brandt said as though that were explanation enough.

''That was foolish of you,'' Steven said, his eyes glowing like a big cat's. ''And incidently that's the last time you're going to lay a hand on anyone. Especially your wife and son.''

''Go on! And who's going to stop me?'' There was a fearsome frown between Brandt's heavy black brows as he stared at Steven.

''You'll be too busy proving you had nothing to do with the North Field mess,'' Steven said.

Brandt jerked back so hard and fast Steven might have thrown acid. His hazel eyes turned mean and murky. ''What the hell are you on about? The place burned down.''

''And how much was the insurance pay out? Forty million

dollars plus. That would split up nicely with a couple of your mates and the guy that lit the blaze?''

''North Field?'' Nat muttered, suddenly losing all colour. ''Dad wasn't involved in that, was he?''

''Fortunately for us all, no,'' Steven clipped off, without looking at his cousin. ''He mightn't always do the right thing but he's not an out-and-out criminal like Brandt here.''

''You keep well clear of me, boy.'' Brandt threatened. ''Don't go shooting off your mouth. The fire was thoroughly investigated. It was an accident.''

''You've got blood on your hands, Brandt. A man died in that fire.''

''A man who shouldn't have been there.'' Brandt smiled a terrible smile. A man ready to defend himself in a minute, ready to pounce like a tiger on anyone he perceived to be a threat.

''There's always someone who *knows*,'' Steven said.

Brandt was very still now. ''Who'd be mad enough to speak out against me?''

Startled and shocked Bronte looked from one to the other. To her mind it was the first time her stepfather actually appeared uneasy.

''Sonia,'' Steven just barely kept his voice level. ''Your first wife, remember? My mother's best friend. They went back many years. Sonia didn't have the courage to stand up to you then. But she has *now*.''

Bronte pressed back against the balustrade for support. She was reeling with all the revelations that rained on her like blows. Knowing her stepfather so well, she saw dread registering in his eyes. ''Sonia accepted a large settlement.'' His voice held as much wariness as anger.

''You mean she was supposed to keep her mouth shut. She did. Whatever you did or said inspired terror in her. But Sonia doesn't care anymore. I've spoken to her. I told her what you were doing to your son. Probably to your wife who just happens to be Bronte's mother.''

"If Sonia speaks out against me she'll regret it deeply."
Brandt snapped his fingers. "So will *you,* Saunders. Who are
you anyway? You're nothing. Your own father cut you off.
I·have all the money in the world, people who take care of
my problems."

"And who's going to take care of *you!*" A woman's ringing voice demanded from behind them. Gilly was standing
in the hallway, Max standing close behind her, her rifle raised
until the butt stock touched her cheek and Brandt was in her
sights. "So this is the infamous Carl Brandt?" she jibed.
"Well, well, well! What, sir, are you doin' on my property
without my permission?"

For a moment there was a big shift in the balance of power.
Even Brandt was silenced. But Steven moved slowly towards
Gilly, speaking persuasively. "It's all right, Gilly. He's not
going to give any trouble. You can put your rifle away."

"Yes, Gilly, put it down. Please, Gilly." Bronte's voice
shook in her throat. She was frightened of what might happen. Gilly had guarded her like a lioness as a child.

The bright red spots on Brandt's swarthy cheeks burned.
"Poor barmy old bat!" He laughed loudly. "They ought to
put her away in a home."

"Careful I don't put *you* away," Gilly responded, looking
as though she was dying to depress the trigger.

Steven continued walking, standing to one side and placing
his hand on the barrel. "Ease up now, Gilly. You can't shoot
him and expect not to land yourself in jail, more's the pity!
We've got a lot of work coming up. Leo has sent a new roll
of sketches you must see."

"The cowardly blaggard!" Gilly fumed, aiming a with-
ering look at Carl Brandt whilst handing over the rifle to
Steven. "I'll never forgive you for what you did to my
Bronte. Or what you've done to young Max here."

"You'd do a whole lot better to mind your own business,"
he shot back. "Keep out of it. It's not your affair. Come here
to me, Max. This is your father speaking."

"Father! How do *I* know?" Max replied to everyone's amazement. "Mum could have been making it up. Are you *sure* I'm your son. I don't look a bit like you, thank crikey. Why is that? I'm not like you in any way. I refuse to go home!" Calling on some inner reserve of courage, Max made his personal declaration of independence. "I refuse to be beaten and bullied and I'd rather die than go back with you. And where is my mother? It's my worry you've done something to her. I'll kill you if you have. She's so beautiful. Why has she stayed with you all these years?"

"Because she was too frightened to go elsewhere, I'd say," Steven answered, his voice and his manner implacable. "You won't find her waiting for you when you get home, Brandt. Both your wife and your son have flown the coop."

"For how long?" Brandt jeered, but for once the bravado rang hollow.

"I'm darned sure I'm not going back with you, either," Nat cried, reaching back to grab Bronte's nerveless hand. "I'm going to stay with my girl."

"The hell you are!" Steven quietly and firmly disengaged Bronte's hand. "This has gone far enough, Nat. You'll have to travel back into town with your friend here—after all you were prepared to help him do his dirty work—then make your own way from there. Ring Dada. He'll send the jet up."

Nat flushed. "Dad will always look after me," he said huffily. "It's more than I can say for you and your father." He couldn't resist pointing that out. He had always been jealous of his difficult, complicated cousin, Steven who had thrown away a brilliant future. "You don't really want me to go, Bronte, do you?" Nat implored of her. "None of this was my fault. I love you. I hated it when you made such a fool of me, but I've missed you too much. Don't worry about my mother. She'll forgive you in time."

"Stuck-up bitch!" So Brandt dismissed Nat's mother.

"Forgive?" Gilly levelled Nat with a glare. "You can't

park yourself here, son. Pack up and get out before I call the police,'' she threatened angrily, heading for the phone.

''Do your worst, Saunders,'' Carl Brandt snarled in Steven's direction. ''It's clear you lost your marbles. Like your mother.''

In front of Bronte's anguished eyes, Steven's lean powerful body went absolutely rigid. His striking face tautened. He looked like he was about to attack. Shocked as she was by his lack of trust in her, Bronte's first thought, nevertheless, was to stop him. If body language was anything to go on her stepfather looked like being beaten to a pulp. Although he deserved it more than anyone she knew it could muddy the waters with an assault charge brought against Steven. That couldn't happen for many reasons. She grasped one of Steven's steely arms, holding on for dear life. ''Leave him, Steven. He's not worth it.''

''No indeed!'' Gilly seconded firmly. ''Fill him full of holes. Save your knuckles.''

Bronte's blood went cold. She held her breath, still gripping Steven's arm, watching in shocked amazement as her stepfather began moving towards the steps.

Was he *going?* It seemed like a miracle straight from heaven.

At the bottom of the steps he made his parting shot. ''What sort of a life is it going to be for you looking over your shoulder, Saunders?'' he growled, all malevolence. ''I haven't finished with you, either, Max, you little hooligan.''

Max, for the first time in his life when his father threatened him, burst out laughing. ''Isn't that a prime case of the pot calling the kettle black? You know what, Gilly.'' He turned to her. ''You should have put a hole in him when you had the chance. He's like someone out of a movie. I ask you, how can he possibly be my father?''

Brandt addressed his son again. ''Your mother's no saint,'' he snarled, ''but she didn't put anything over me, just

Bronte's poor fool of a father. You're *my* son however much you want to be someone else's. Remember that, Max.''

A surge of adrenaline propelled Max across the verandah. ''I'm my own man,'' he shouted after his father.

''And we're very proud of you,'' Bronte went to him, hugging him emotionally.

''Aye, aye,'' Gilly seconded, cracking her knuckles. She walked to the balustrade, gazing in astonished admiration at Steven. ''Where in the world did you get that helicopter, Steve?''

''Gee, you can fly one?'' Max's eyes flew to his newfound friend.

''I borrowed it from a developer friend. I can't keep it too long, I'm afraid.'' Steven watched narrow eyed as Brandt and his cousin drove away, Brandt thrusting his hand out the window to give the usual obscene signal. ''I'd like to make sure your father makes it safely back to town, Max. Would you like to come with me?''

''Would I ever!'' Max was thrilled.

Steven sought Bronte's gaze but she wouldn't look at him. She was trying too hard to sort out a deluge of mixed emotions. ''If no one has a complaint,'' he said sardonically, ''I'll bring Max back in the 4WD later. I'm not expecting any trouble, but if it's okay I'll stay the night.''

Gilly touched his hand and smiled. She'd forgive him anything Bronte thought. She, on the other hand, went on the attack feeling wronged and betrayed. ''Are you sure there isn't more to tell, Steven *Saunders,* or are we going to get it in dribs and drabs. I find that completely humiliating. You haven't been married and divorced, I wonder? I wouldn't put it past you.''

''Bronte, love!'' Gilly remonstrated, trying to save Bronte from herself.

''That's okay, Gilly.'' Steven's tone was composed. ''No, I'm single, Bronte.'' He laid an arm around Max's thin shoulders compelling him down the steps. "And the name's *Randolph*."

Man and boy strode away like a pair of adventurers to the bright yellow helicopter. "Come back, Steven, and you and Bronte can have a good talk," Gilly called after him.

"Beginning with why he lied to me," Bronte said bitterly.

"He must have thought it best to say nothing," Gilly defended Steven. "That's not lying, is it?"

"A technicality, Gilly."

"All I know is whatever he's got on your stepfather it saved the day." Gilly gave a curt nod of approval.

They remained lost in thought as the rotor blades began to whirl, the rotation gaining power and speed as they lifted off vertically before executing a half turn towards the coast.

"So that's how it's done then!" Gilly said with immense satisfaction. "Hell of a way to take a trip and I'm going to do it. Over to the islands with Steven. Never know what you can do until you try. I tell you, girl, if I was fifty years younger I'd be giving you a run for your money. Steven makes me feel, I dunno, damned near young!"

"So I've noticed!" Bronte groaned loudly. "I may not be your only competition, either. There's still Christine."

"Better get cracking then." Gilly snorted. "She's beautiful and smart I grant you, and it's really awful she's fallen in love with him, but nothing will come of it."

"How do you know?"

Gilly laughed. "One of the reasons I love you is you have no vanity at all. Christine will find a suitable man to marry but believe me it won't be Steven. He's yours if you want 'im!"

Bronte swallowed hard. "You're making it sound far too easy, Gilly. I may be powerfully attracted to him and maybe, just maybe, he's powerfully attracted to me, but how long does *that* last?"

"Hell, as long as you want, girl. Long enough to get married and have kids. Make a life. Most people never get to experience powerful attraction. Count yourself lucky.''

"It would have been nice if he'd seen fit to take me into his confidence," Bronte said, still inconsolable.

"Can you ease up a little?" Gilly dropped a hand on her shoulder. "He'd have got around to it. Now you sit down over there. You've had a bad fright. I'll make us both a nice cup of my coffee. I've freshly roasted it. Should make the perfect cup."

"Don't you think you roast it a bit long?" Bronte suggested. Gilly's coffee was so strong and bitter it would have kept Rip Van Winkle awake.

Gilly laughed. "You know what Steven, that rascal calls it? The devil's drink."

"He's a devil himself!" Bronte declared. "He should have told me right off he knew my stepfather, let alone he's Nat's cousin. I feel like a rug had been pulled out from under my feet. I want a man who is prepared to share his deepest, darkest secrets with me, not deceive me."

"I bet there's plenty you haven't told him," Gilly said, with the air of presenting a legal argument. "Besides, you weren't all that sweet to him at the beginning, as I recall." Her black eyes softened. "You wouldn't remember, you're way too young—but there was a movie many years ago called *Saunders of the River*. The star was Paul Robeson, the great American bass-baritone. Lovely film." She shoved a wicker chair out of her way. "Steven Saunders." She tried the name on her tongue. "I think that suits him perfectly."

"Oh Gilly!" Bronte wailed. "You'd take it in your stride if you found out he'd had a sex change and was previously Stephanie. Anyway he has huge problems with being Steven Saunders. That's why he changed his name."

"Steven is a young man who's been wounded," Gilly said, a frown appearing on her face as she dwelt on it. "He can't get past something his father did. Unless *you're* thinking of making it through life on your own—which is really hard—I wouldn't get stuck on your high horse, my girl. The fact is Steven has proved not only our friend but Max's saviour. I saw that big windbag Brandt deflate before my very eyes.''

''And who is Sonia?'' Bronte asked, coming to her next point.

''Let's start off with the fact she was your stepfather's first wife.''

''I wonder when number two will pop up?''

''Be patient. All will be revealed in time,'' Gilly said.

''And where has my mother gone?'' Bronte agonised. ''Why hasn't she tried to contact me?''

Gilly sniffed and walked briskly through the front door. ''I wouldn't worry too much about your mother, child,'' she called back. ''Miranda's probably booked herself into Palazzo Versace on the Gold Coast. And if what young Max told me is anything to go by, she won't be on her own.''

CHAPTER NINE

IT WAS close to ten at night before they heard from Miranda. Gilly really did have psychic powers because the opulent Palazzo Versace on Queensland's tourist strip of the Gold Coast was exactly where Miranda was camping out.

"I had a long talk with your friend Steven," she told a dumbfounded Bronte.

"You're kidding!"

"No, hasn't he mentioned it?"

Bronte didn't tell her mother she wasn't talking to Steven.

"Anyway I want you and Max to know I've already met with my lawyers. I'm filing for a divorce."

"So who's the guy?" Bronte, her father never far from her mind, asked somewhat bitterly.

"What guy?" Miranda was all affronted innocence. "Ye Gods, *what* guy? I'm ringing to tell you and Max I'm safe and well—or well enough—and all you can be is sarcastic?"

"I'm sorry, Mum." Bronte didn't care if Miranda objected to "Mum" or not.

"You have such a sharp tongue. I worry about you, Bronte, I really do."

Was this a latter day conversion?

Miranda wanted to speak to Max but Max, overcome by relief and exhaustion, was safely asleep in a big soft downy bed having told them he was never going to leave. Miranda said she would ring again. She redeemed herself further by asking after Gilly. She sent her love. It didn't sound like Bronte's mother at all.

After the call, Bronte tapped on Gilly's bedroom door. Gilly too had retired, but not long before Miranda's call.

"It's open, love," Gilly called. "Who was that on the

phone?'' She switched on the bedside lamp and sat up, looking in the dim light strangely *young,* her white hair in a thick plait.

"That was Mum otherwise known as Miranda." Bronte delivered the news, pleased Gilly was wearing the blue satin pyjamas she had bought for her as an alternative to the kind of nighties Gilly could never take to a hospital. "I'm able to tell you your prediction about her hiding out at the Palazzo Versace is spot-on. Congratulations. It's a wonder you haven't been tempted to go on television. Miranda didn't say who was with her being the soul of discretion, but she did say she's filing for divorce. She's seen her lawyers. Better yet she seems to have swallowed a good dose of redemption I can only hope will last her all her life. She sends you her *love!*''

"Good grief!" Gilly violently whacked her pillows. "Are you sure it was Miranda?"

"I told you. She's turned into a sweet, caring person. She's spoken to Steven, did you know?"

There was a slight pause while Gilly rearranged the bed clothes. "He took Max and I into his confidence as you made it perfectly clear you weren't going to speak to him."

"It's the only way I know to make a point," Bronte defended herself. "By the way the rifle wasn't loaded, was it?" she asked dryly.

Gilly gave a huge yawn and lay back on the pillows. "Brandt didn't know that."

"Neither did Steven yet he walked right up to you."

"He's got plenty of guts like someone else I know," Gilly said. "Why don't you go talk to him and let me go to sleep?"

Bronte walked to the door, blowing a kiss. "Love you, Gilly. Sweet dreams."

"Love you too, little angel," Gilly called. "I can read you like a book."

* * *

The night couldn't have been called black. It couldn't have been called dark. The moon and the stars so lit the sky the heavens were indigo. The same moonlight drew lacy patterns through the trees onto the grass; made of Oriole's volcanic hill a cardboard cut-out: a sharp peak and a rounded hump overshadowing the homestead.

In the kitchen Bronte poured herself a glass of cold white wine and took it out to the rear verandah. She had no idea where Steven was. Probably he too had gone to bed. She could have cut him a break but she didn't. Her feelings were too mixed up.

Let's face it, kiddo. You're on your own.

Victim of her sharp tongue. But the fact was she felt very distressed Steven hadn't confided in her. Her feelings for him hadn't changed. She was still madly in love with him, but nevertheless she felt unhappy and uncertain. She'd endured such a dysfunctional life she wasn't going to change overnight. She had to have a man she could trust. A man who was the same person she thought he was. She couldn't cope with multiple identities.

Was that too much to ask?

White bougainvillea, like a bridal veil stretched right across and down the sides of the wide awning. The gardens near her, awash with gardenias, frangipani, oleanders, the Kahili Ginger and the spectacular African Wintersweet flooded the perfect night with fragrance so deep it was possible to drown in it.

She settled herself in a rattan armchair and took a long sip of her wine, set it down. The chill would go off it quickly in the tropical heat. She lay back watching the stars turn on their brilliant display. Was she imagining it or were they multicoloured, twinkling white-hot, red and blue. Her eyes filled in the pattern of the Southern Cross. The constellation she had gazed up at all her life. The copper moon must have the wind behind it because it was sailing like a galleon across the sky.

Where was *her* life going? She couldn't imagine. Nothing had ever been the same since the day she'd met Steven. His impact on her had been immense like a powerful chemical reaction; pheromones released by the male to capture the female? Whatever it was it drew them inexorably together.

It would have been nice to look at all Leo's sketches tonight; his early drafts for the landscaping, but she'd been too proud. Make that pig-headed.

She never saw Steven standing in the shadows until he spoke to her. "What do you see when you're looking up there?" he asked. He pulled up a matching rattan chair near her and sat down.

"You startled me." She put a hand to the leaping pulse in her throat.

"Sorry. I kept quiet so you wouldn't run away. Why are you running, Bronte?"

"You really don't have to ask me that, do you?" She didn't turn her head, but she could see him quite clearly. Feel him. Smell him like a lioness would her mate. He made all her senses come alive. Even angry with him he thrilled her. That gave him an enormous advantage.

"You said yourself, Bronte, what's happening between us has been darn near fearfully *sudden*. With so little passage of time it's been hard to catch up. For both of us. At the beginning, because of the talk of a partnership with Gilly, you were predisposed to distrust me. Your trust became very important to me. What do you suppose would have happened had I introduced myself as Nat's cousin?"

"I would have handled it." She caught her flowing hair back into its large tortoiseshell clasp.

"You *wouldn't!*" A flat contradiction.

"All right, I wouldn't." She glanced at him briefly. His shirt glowed palely. His handsome face was in shadow. "It's all so weird, our meeting up. Why did you come up here, to North Queensland, in the first place? Why so far from home?"

"Fancy *you* asking me that," Steven retorted with grim

humour. "Queensland is a favourite getaway. It's where it's all happening, a top tourist destination and it's still frontier country. Like you, I wanted to put as much distance between my family and myself as possible. I was like Max. I wanted to be my own man. I think I am, and with precious little assistance except for my inheritance from my mother. That kept me afloat as she meant it to."

"What happened to your mother?" Bronte asked, knowing she was on very emotional ground. "Why do you hate your father so much?"

"I don't usually talk about it, Bronte." His voice was low and clipped. "It doesn't help."

"You don't usually talk about anything." There was sadness and regret in her voice. "That's what bothers me. Now might be a good time to start communicating. I want to know what goes on in your *mind*, Steven."

"When I've spent years of my life keeping it to myself?" He shook his head.

"Tell me this. How did you get around to speaking to *my* mother? How did you even know where to contact her?"

"Where else but the family mansion, Bronte? Your mother was distraught. For the first time Brandt had marked her face. She was too ashamed to tell anyone. I managed to convince her to pack up a few things and get out. There was a good chance worse might happen to her. She didn't really need any prompting. She intends to divorce him. She's known for years she ought to do something, but he's had too powerful a hold on her. His rage at Max's defection brought it all to a head. She was terrified for Max."

"But she didn't think to warn us he was coming?" Bronte asked in a rising voice.

"She's *your* mother, Bronte." Steven shrugged. "I expect she's gone a lifetime putting herself first. She'd be more concerned with making her own getaway."

"Not to a safe house, but a really swish hotel," Bronte responded tartly. "At least she's safe!" She was unable to relax in his presence, so many emotions came into play. "What's going to happen to him, do you know?"

Steven's tone hardened. "Once tipped off, the corporate regulator will be on to him. They'll raid his home and his offices, and those of anyone connected to the scandal. The whole sorry case will be re-investigated. It was well over ten years ago, but many things have changed especially with the cyber sleuths."

"What do they do?" Bronte turned her head.

"They can recover deleted and hidden files—files stay on computers even when you think you've deleted them. In point of fact you've only deleted the reference to the file. They can also conduct searches for secret bank accounts."

"So most of us are leaving a trail behind us on our computers?" Bronte asked, thinking of the files, harmless enough, she'd confidently believed she'd deleted from her home computer.

"That's right." Steven nodded. "These forensic computing experts are *smart*. They begin by creating binary images of all the data on the hard drives. They then probe the images using special software. If they can build a case criminal charges will be laid. He'll get the best legal team behind him. Chances are he could get off. The courts aren't always about justice."

"And your mother's friend, Sonia, his first wife?"

"If the case is dragged out I don't know if Sonia will survive it. Recently she was diagnosed with an inoperable brain tumour. She's perfectly lucid now but tragically she will deteriorate. The prognosis isn't good. The thing is she doesn't fear Brandt anymore. Facing certain death, she's let go of fear. So in the end, it looks like Sonia, the victim of an abusive marriage, is going to nail him."

"Max will have to change his name. Like you," Bronte said soberly.

"I like Randolph. It's a good name. It's mine." His tone firmed.

"Is there *no* chance of a reconciliation with your father and brother?"

Steven looked off into the starry night. "With my brother, maybe. With my father, never. He's considered a pillar of the establishment and treated accordingly. But when my mother lay upstairs dying and in horrendous pain, my father was bringing his mistress into the house. She's only two years older than Lyall. It was an appalling thing to do."

"It was an appalling thing for *her* to do as well." Bronte commented, thinking how his home life must have been.

"My mother couldn't hold on after that," he said bleakly. "Our fool of a housekeeper told her, though I've no idea why, because she loved my mother. Perhaps she thought my mother should know. Anyway my father sacked her. He and his mistress deserved one another. My father fully expected us to countenance his actions. He's a handsome virile man and my mother had been ill for so long. I know it was hard, but he didn't even have the decency to see his mistress privately. He had to bring her into our home. It was so cruel. Lyall hated it as much as I did but he knew life would get a lot tougher if he didn't go along with everything my father wanted. It was obvious the mistress was in my father's life to stay."

"He married her?" Bronte asked quietly.

Steven nodded. "They have a daughter. My little half sister. I've never seen her. I believe he dotes on her."

"At least she'll have an easier life than you did." Bronte stood up, feeling sad and deeply troubled. "I think I'll go to bed. It's been an eventful day. I'm like Max, God love him. Too much emotion has worn me out." She gave him a brief injured glance.

"I'll stay here for a while," he said, his voice low in his throat.

The sound of it made her legs go wobbly. She had to leave before she made a total fool of herself. "Okay," she managed to say. He was seated directly in front of a pillar, so she had to walk round him, not realizing her beauty was a teasing torment.

His hand reached for her, caught her like a hook.

She was crushed in his arms. Everything was heat and light. The absolute connection of their mouths, desperate with passion.

"You mean so much to me, Bronte," he groaned.

"I want to believe that." She pressed her head back against his shoulder, the starlight caught in her eyes.

"What can I do to convince you?" His hand, fingers splayed, caressed her breast. He pushed the narrow strap of her sundress aside seeking her naked flesh.

He was touching her in such a way the breath almost cut off in her throat. Desire swept through her, catching her up like a leaf in the wind. She was frantic with longing, snuggling even closer into his body. Wherever he touched her there were sparks. His hand ranged down over her bent legs, to her ankles, long stroking movements, then up again, surging hungrily beneath the hem of her skirt, brushing over her thighs, but stopping short of her quivering core. Still she felt the sharp sensations, the astounding arousal. The feeling was exquisite, the sexual energy that was pouring from him to her. Her head fell back. He was mouthing her nipples causing her sensation-flooded body to writhe. She needed him desperately.

"I can't go this far and not have you!"

His voice reverberated through her.

"Spend the night with me, Bronte," he begged.

"We *can't!* You know we can't." She was trembling all over, but acutely mindful Gilly and Max would be right down the hall.

"I'd do anything to have you." His emotions too intense to withstand, he swept up from his chair, taking the weight of her as though it were nothing.

She clung to him, wrapping her arms around his neck, panicked by the sheer force of passion that emanated from his body. She doubted she could control him. It was hard enough controlling herself. But she dared not give in. "Steven, we can't," she pleaded, her skin burning.

"Do you *want* to?" He held her higher, staring into her luminous eyes.

"Yes, damn you!" Her resistance was growing weaker by the second. "But it's hard with Gilly and Max in the house. I feel like a kid breaking the rules."

"Okay, I suppose I can relate to that," he groaned. "But it's so…so…*enraging!*" He lowered her to the floor, pulling her body hard up against him. "You slept with Nat, didn't you?"

"Does that make you angry?" She searched his expression.

"It sure does." He pulled back her long hair, draping it around his wrist.

"I'm older and I hope wiser now," she said, shakily. "Nat was a terrible choice. He wasn't even *my* choice."

"But you went along with it?" His voice was laced with a jealousy he couldn't hide.

"It was nice for a while to bask in my mother's approval." Bronte tried to explain. "Even my brute of a stepfather approved."

"But then you did get out of it alone," he said as though she had at least passed the test.

"Yes, thank goodness," she muttered fervently. "I can feel you're angry with me."

He lifted her face to him. "What am I supposed to feel?" He didn't wait for an answer but bent his head kissing her hard. "I'll tell you one thing, Bronte McAllister. I wouldn't take this torture from any other woman but you. I want you, and it's got to be soon. You choose the place and the time."

A week passed. They heard nothing from anyone except Miranda who sent e-mailed messages for Bronte and Max to join her.

They declined politely, putting pressure on Miranda to join them on Oriole for Christmas.

"She probably thinks we'll catch a snake and bake it," Gilly joked.

Miranda could not commit herself. She'd met up with a very nice man who'd taken her under his wing. Purely platonic of course. They regarded one another as friends. Besides, the long term weather forecast predicted a few cyclones up there. Were they aware of it?

Very much so. There was an excellent tropical cyclone warning system in place. The earliest cyclone in any season had been Ines in November '73. Australia's greatest natural disaster occurred on Christmas Day 1973 when Cyclone Tracy destroyed Darwin. In the tropical North most cyclones formed in the Coral Sea between December, which they were already into, and April at the latest although Western Australia had been hit by a cyclone as late as May in 1988.

Gilly and Bronte found it wonderful to be able to drive on the sealed road leading in and out of the plantation. They had Steven to thank for that. They also had to thank him for befriending Max to the extent of taking Max about with him on his business travels which involved a good deal of land exploration. Within a short space of time Max had gained weight and a golden tan against which his extraordinary eyes sparkled. When Gilly asked him what he thought of Steven the answer was a beaming: "First rate!"

They all pored over the beautifully drawn, coloured and detailed landscape designs Leo had forwarded to Steven, spread out over the dining room table. Leo called them mere drafts but the plans gave them a wonderful overview of the famous designer's vision for Oriole. With modern machinery it was possible to create even large scale landscapes very quickly—Bronte marvelled at what had been achieved with human labour in centuries gone by—but it was essential Gilly and Bronte liked and understood what Leo proposed before the actual landscape sculpting took place. All being well, Leo proposed April of the following year and the onset of the Dry. With any luck he might be able to pop in on them for a Christmas drink. He'd let them know.

"What do you say I chuck school?" Max proposed, finding everything about the flamboyant tropics, his new lifestyle and the proposed venture exciting.

"Forget it, pal!" Steven said firmly. "Education is everything. You're clever. Once you're through university you can choose a career."

"I'm not going back to my father," Max vowed. "I don't care where I live as long as it's here!"

Gilly and Bronte weren't left out of the expeditions. True to his word Steven organised a helicopter trip to one of the beautiful luxury island resorts. The view from the air was superlative! The wonderful colourations in the crystal clear waters, ranged from a sparkling aquamarine, through jade to turquoise, and cobalt to intense ultramarine. The deeper the water the deeper the blue intensified. The Great Barrier Reef, the greatest coral formation in the world, spread over a phenomenal area of some eighty thousand square miles along the east coast of Queensland and up into the Torres Strait with thousands of small islands and coral cays. They were heading towards Royal Hayman, rated among the top three island resorts in the world. There was time for a swim in the lagoon, alas no snorkelling amid the fantastic coral gardens with all the gorgeous little tropical fish flitting about—that would have to wait for another time, but a sumptuous buffet lunch and afterwards a walk around the island.

As she was trying to decide over the marvellous array of buffet food, hot and cold featuring the wonderful seafood of the Reef waters, Bronte could feel someone staring at her.

It was Christine.

Hell!

It was impossible to be rude. Bronte summoned up all her good manners, giving the other woman a smile and a little wave. At various stages around the buffet tables and at the hot food section were Gilly, pink cheeked and happy, followed by Steven with a chattering Max who had never left his side even when they went for a swim. The swimmers included Gilly who had no qualms whatsoever about showing off her seventy-six-year-old body, tall and spare and in considerably better condition than her costume.

Mercifully Christine couldn't join them, mouthing she was on a day trip with friends though as usual she craved a private word with Steven. Lying in wait for him she drew him aside delicately.

"Who's that?" Max asked, round eyed. "She's a doll!"

"Sure is," Bronte agreed laconically. "It's tough to be beautiful." She watched out of the corner of her eye as Christine constantly made little butterfly movements with her hands, one occasionally alighting on Steven's bare arm.

"I hope I'm going to get to meet her," said Max, adolescent hormones rising. "Steven must be a huge hit with the women."

"Christine is Steven's partner in the motel," Gilly harrumphed. "Partners don't count."

Finally Christine allowed Steven to go on his way, smiling and waving at the rest of them seated at the table.

Max waved back enthusiastically. "Gosh, she's sooo amazing!"

"How would you like that plate of oysters in your lap?" his sister asked, for some reason wanting to kill him.

"Pardon me!" Max scoffed. "You're not going to marry him, are you?"

"I'm not marrying *anyone!*" Bronte declared.

The brilliantly fine weather eventually broke. Spectacular thunderstorms were almost a daily occurrence waiting until late afternoon to turn on their awesome displays. Almost all were short lived. The sun came out again thirty minutes later, to blaze brilliantly. There was a brief mauve dusk like a curtain coming down at intermission and star filled nights.

Bronte found herself going slightly troppo. She couldn't think of another word. Cat on a hot tin roof came to mind.

"What's the matter?" Gilly asked as she prowled restlessly.

She could hardly answer: "Does sex starved mean anything to you?" Sex was the one word not in Gilly's vocabulary.

Steven, it dawned on her, was playing hard to get. Which was ridiculous. Was he paying her out? Was he angry about Nat?

"You've got it bad, haven't you, girlie?" Gilly put her arm around Bronte's shoulder and hugged her.

Desperately bad, Bronte thought, but wild horses wouldn't have got it out of her.

Friday morning's paper carried a small piece about the old corporate scandal involving the mysterious fire.

"It's started!" Max observed quietly to Bronte. "I should be able to find some pity in my heart for him, but I can't. He gave us all a rotten time."

In the afternoon, while Max and Gilly went off on another of their companionable tramps through the incredibly lush forest with its great diversity of plant life, Bronte took a necessary trip into town. She needed more clothing and so did Max. It was doubtful indeed if either of them could retrieve their wardrobes let alone their possessions from the Brandt mansion. In that she was wrong, but it would take time.

The town catered to the tourist trade so she had no difficulty finding good quality holiday wear at various outlets. There were two excellent boutiques that carried plenty of the more upmarket designer labels for herself, so she had a fruitful relaxing time making all her purchases. A stop off at "Pauline's" to buy handmade chocolates, chocolate fudge and coconut ice for Gilly who had a weakness for sweets. A couple of new lipsticks for herself from the pharmacy. She never had to go to the expense of buying skin cleansers and moisturizers. Gilly's creams were as gentle as they were effective at a fraction of the price of the products of the leading cosmetic houses that charged big time for added fragrance and presentation.

She was coming out of the pharmacy with her purchases and Gilly's prescription eye drops when she ran into Christine, who was going in.

"Bronte, how are you?" Christine's mouth smiled, her eyes were hidden behind her designer sunglasses.

Both women moved away from the entrance back onto the pavement. Christine was wearing a yellow dress that threw off light, yellow sandals on her feet, a very pretty straw bag decorated with clumps of yellow and white flowers over her arm. In the sweltering humidity she looked as cool as a lily.

"I'm fine, Christine and you?" Bronte got her tongue working. She would bet money Christine would have something vaguely upsetting to say.

"I keep well," Christine trilled. "And busy. The two I think are related. What brings you into town?" She lifted her head to gaze at an increasingly ominous sky. "I fear you'll run into a storm on your way home."

Bronte frowned. "That was quick. It didn't look anywhere near as bad an hour ago." Of course it happened like that. She should know.

"And your family, they are well?" Christine asked sweetly. "Steven tells me you have your half brother with you?"

"Yes." Bronte smiled. "You would have seen him that day on Hayman. His name is Max."

"Aah, yes, Max. He and Steven have become good friends?"

"Steven has been very nice to him." Bronte stood by the truth.

Christine nodded wisely. "As he's been nice to you. As

he was nice to me. Steven knows exactly what he wants and how to go after it. It's a quality I admire.''

"I'm not quite following you, Christine." Bronte brooded on that answer.

"I'm sure you are. You do not strike me as unintelligent."

"That's good to know," Bronte said briskly. "I don't look on you as unintelligent, either."

Christine opened her lovely mouth to retort but Bronte cut her off. "What you're saying is—forgive me if I'm wrong— Steven deliberately cultivated me and now my brother to please my aunt?"

Christine took off her sunglasses and looked directly into Bronte's eyes. "Generally speaking, don't these things happen? It's called public relations. Steven badly wanted Miss McAllister as a partner," she offered by way of explanation.

"Surely he's doing well enough in the enterprise he shares with you?" Bronte's tone was sharpening by the minute.

Christine laughed lightly, putting her sunglasses back on again. "Steven mightn't speak to his father, but he has his father's genes. His father heads a most prestigious law firm and Steven is driven to succeed. His plans, like all our plans, affects his behaviour."

"He wouldn't thank you to hear you call him an opportunist. You know about Steven's alienation from his family?" Bronte asked, beginning to wonder if Steven had lied and lied to her about this woman.

"Of course." Christine sounded amazed Bronte didn't know that. "Steven and I go back years. He confided in me. I confided in him. In this way we became close. Many young women have tried to fasten on to Steven, Miss McAllister, but he always comes back to me."

"Is it all right if I call you Ms Ching Yee?" Bronte retaliated. "Steven comes back to you as someone he respects and admires. His partner."

"Wrong!" Christine's figure stiffened. "I am far more than that, Miss McAllister. It is just no good for you to get up your hopes. I seek only to do you a favour. I hate to say it, but you could be badly hurt. Now if you will excuse me, I have purchases to make, then I must return to the restaurant. Even you must wonder what Steven would ever do without me?''

"Hire some very well qualified person to take over," Bronte shot back.

Last word or not Bronte felt deeply upset. Her and her insecurities! Would she ever be free of them? Would Nat have wanted to marry her if she hadn't been the mega-rich Carl Brandt's stepdaughter? Men were known to pursue potential heiresses. Her stepfather had always put on a good show of affection for her. In public. A lot of people had been fooled. Her own mother had made a practice of going after rich men even if she had taken it in stages. People married for convenience, security and position all the time. They weren't all love matches. Many settled for second best rather than be left on their lonesome. For a lot of people a great sex life wasn't the most important thing in marriage. Passion evaporated, sometimes overnight. She had the proof. What feelings she'd had for Nat had done that.

Okay so Steven wanted her? Once he got her he could very easily drop her. Look what had happened to Anne Boleyn. Men's approach to sex was very different to a woman's. Sex was all they ever thought about. It did a man no real harm to have a wife and a mistress. Presumably the mistress made a nice change.

Was a driven man the right man for her? She reminded herself Steven had never said he *loved* her. He'd only gone as far as *want*. Want without love put her on the defensive.

Bronte fretted all the way back to the ute. She could just about afford to buy Gilly a reliable secondhand car for Christmas though Gilly who drove like she was in a rally would be safer in a ten ton lorry. By the time she reached the old utility, the first heavy spits of rain were coming down, striking the hot road and the pavements with an audible sizzle. One could fry eggs out there.

Why had she left it so long? She couldn't drive home in this. She'd have to wind the windows up and there was no such thing as air conditioning in the ancient vehicle. On top of that the wipers wouldn't be terribly effective in heavy rain. She sighed in complete exasperation. Her only option was to wait it out. It was a good thing the storm would cool the air down.

Bronte unlocked the door and tossed her parcels on the passenger seat and the floor. A massive clap of thunder gave her such a fright she bumped her head on the window.

"Damn!"

"Bronte!" A voice yelled to her.

She looked up to see Steven dodge a couple of cars in his race across the street. "Boy did I pick the right moment!" His mahogany hair was damp, as well as the shoulders of his shirt. His tanned polished skin was sleek with rain drops. He looked marvellous. So vivid, so handsome, so alert, he took her breath away. "You can't drive home in this."

"I don't intend to." A wind borne gust of rain hit them, almost blowing her off her feet.

"We've got time to make it to my place." He looked up at the lurid sky. "Hail could be a real concern. Five—ten minutes at the outside—all hell will break loose. You can follow me or leave the ute here and come in my car."

"I'm quite okay, Steven," she said in a self-reliant sort of way. "I'll go get myself a cup of coffee or something. Wait it out."

"Don't be so damned stubborn," he said, his green eyes flashing. "This is no time to dig your heels in, Bronte. Get right back into that ute and follow me. Gilly won't like it very much if it's hail damaged."

"What does it matter?" She gave a short laugh. "The darn thing is falling to bits."

"Why do you waste time arguing?" he cried impatiently.

"There's no doubt in my mind this is going to be as bad a storm as we've had up to date. If you value your own safety you'll come *now*."

"Okay, okay. Keep your shirt on." Feeling foolish she moved behind the wheel, shivering slightly at the sudden drop in temperature.

Ten minutes later they were safe inside his garage, entering the house through a rear door.

Incandescent light was pouring through the floor to ceiling windows as lightning hit the earth in obliterating flashes. Fronds of the tall palms in the garden were being lashed by the searing wind. The sea was wild. An immensity of churning water the same lurid colour as the sky, charcoal shot through with rising waves of silver, purple and green-black. Close to the shore fortified by great boulders white spray exploded twenty and more feet into the air.

It was a seascape so stunning, so majestic, for a moment Bronte just stood there with a catch in her throat, glorying in the power of nature. Outside the wind whistled and howled, threatening to invade the house, the violent rain driving itself against the plate glass windows. Flying clouds raced across the heavens. The thunder was terrible but the lightning was far more frightening. Minutes went by as they stood mesmerized by the wild display. There was no gentling of rain or wind. As Steven had predicted this one was bad. At such moments Bronte's mind was given to thoughts of Gilly's and Max's safety. Not that she should worry. Gilly had lived through such displays and far worse all her life. Oriole, low set homestead hugging the earth, in the lee of its volcanic hill, had always stood firm.

Just as they began to think they would escape the hail, it came down, scores of sparkling icy chunks decorating the grass. They could hear it crashing savagely on the roof. Rivulets of liquid silver were running down the tall windows. Streams more tumbling off the roof as the guttering lost the battle to contain the volume of water.

Safe inside the house Bronte was swamped by excitement. A huge glossy wave, livid green at the centre, exploded onto the rocks beneath.

"Oh my!" She made an odd little sound in her throat.

"You're not frightened, are you?" Steven closed the distance between them as another bolt of lightning dazzled the gun-metal sky with astonishing brilliance.

"No," she whispered.

"The house was built with cyclones in mind." He folded her into his arms, making her blood *sing*. "Are you worried we're alone?"

"I'm glad to be alone," she freely admitted, "but I need you to tell me what you want of me, Steven?"

"Live with me." He stared down at her, his hunger growing steadily.

"As what, your mistress?"

"I'd grab you anyway," he said wryly. "But it just so happens I don't want you for a mistress." He bent to kiss her, his body thrumming with desire.

Bronte spoke quickly before she was lost. "It's Christine's job, after all."

He drew back instantly, his expression taut. "What in hell are you talking about?"

"I know more than you think, Steven." She spoke severely, though she was on the verge of tears.

"You don't know a darn thing," he said crisply. "No, I'm not letting you go, so don't try pulling away. Explain yourself, Bronte."

"Not me. *You,*" she protested. "You could start by being honest."

"Isn't this honest enough?" He didn't bother to disguise his impatience. He caught her mouth up with his, kissing her until soft little cries came out of her, and all her hostility evaporated in blinding heat. "I'm here with *you,*" he muttered against her hot cheek. "How can you believe such nonsense?"

"I've seen the two of you together." Her heart was beating so fast her breath caught.

Her jealousy excited him, sent his hunger raging. "It's *you* I want to be with, Bronte," he said urgently. "It's you I want to touch. It's you I want to make love to. In fact, you're not leaving here until I do."

He fell to kissing her until her head lolled back under the weight of his passion. Then he lifted her yearning body carrying her through the house, up the curving stairway to the huge master bedroom overlooking the tempest tossed sea.

He lay her on the bed, staring down at her with infinite desire. Her eyes were like jewels. Her long dark hair fell like silk over the bed cushions. Her delicate slender body was trembling. "How did you get the idea Christine was my mistress?" he asked.

She flushed deeper. "She loves you."

"Loneliness," he explained. "Her loneliness has been bad but I've done nothing to offer Christine any hope of a relationship, Bronte. I've given comfort when she needed it. I see Christine as a good friend. I told you."

"You told her about your family. You didn't tell me." There was no denying the hurt in her voice.

He let his eyes rest on her. His hands went to her narrow waist. "Must we talk about Christine? I only want to talk about us. Christine and I exchanged confidences at a time when we were both at a low point in our lives. I've known Christine for years. Don't you think if I'd been in love with her I'd have done something about it before now?"

Bronte's carefully stacked argument seemed to be falling apart. She had no wish to embarrass Christine by repeating her claims to Steven. "I guess so," she said.

"I *know* so." He gave her a mocking smile.

Her flesh was melting. Tremors ran through her. Colour washed into her skin. Steven lowered himself to the side of the bed. He lifted the edge of her tank top, his green eyes looking deeply, intensely into hers. She put up her arms like a child allowing him to peel it off her. She felt strangely naked but filled with a wild joy. Abruptly she sat up. At a rush, she started to unbutton his shirt, so she could touch his bare skin, her fingers normally so nimble making such a botch of it that he had to rip the shirt off himself. He was six feet plus of tanned skin, bone and muscle, with powerful shoulders.

There was no waiting now for either of them. Their eagerness for each other was mounting to fever pitch. They made love in a tangle of clothes. Progressed to nakedness. Skin on skin. Everything was perfect. At some point a golden ray of sunlight slashed through the windows signalling the storm they had been oblivious to had blown out to sea.

Steven lifted himself on his strong arms as he entered her, moving slowly, carefully, watching her enraptured face so he could adjust his rhythms to hers. He was highly aroused, his climax exquisitely not far off, but he wanted her to experience the ultimate pleasure he could give her. He knew he wanted this woman with a rare passion. He knew he *loved* her. Passion and a profound tenderness poured out of him. Only Bronte could fill him with such emotions.

Her lovely eyes opened, met his. "I love you, Steven," she murmured and laid a gentle hand against his cheek. "I love *this!*"

"Marry me." He didn't know what he'd do if she said no.

Bronte felt her whole body glowing. Joy moved through her like an actual beam of light. It was extraordinary. "Forever and ever and ever?" Her smile blossomed like a rose.

"I made my choice the day I met you." His voice was deep with feeling. "It's til death do us part."

"Then the answer is yes, Steven." Little tears spilled out the corner of her eyes. "Yes, yes, yes! I've waited so long for someone to love!"

"Nothing to cry about, my darling," he said with gentle humour, brushing the tears away.

"I need to say goodbye to the past, Steven," she replied.

"I know, my precious girl. But I'm your future. You're mine."

In the full blaze of this wonderful knowledge, Bronte closed her arms around his neck, her eyelashes falling like black crescents against her cheeks. "Fill me," she begged passionately. "Fill me with your love. Take me to Heaven."

It is possible for a man and woman in love.

Passion has its own magic. Love gives us wings.

EPILOGUE

Christmas
Oriole Plantation

AFTERWARDS they voted it the best Christmas ever, though it wasn't without its mind blowing shocks. Bronte wore her beautiful engagement ring for the first time. With her morning glory eyes it had to be a blue stone but Steven had surprised and delighted her not with the usual sapphire but a magnificent emerald cut tanzanite surrounded by glittering diamonds.

"Now that's my idea of an engagement ring!" Gilly exclaimed when Bronte first showed it to her. "All the happiness in the world to you, my darling girl!" she said, giving her great-niece a big hug. "This is a true love match. I couldn't be happier. I was the one to bring you and Steven together after all!"

Toasts to the young lovers were drunk in vintage champagne. Steven spoke lovingly, heartbreakingly, of winning his beloved's caged heart, a flame burning in his eyes.

"Steven, Steven, what a lovely speech!" Gilly cried while Bronte stood locked in her lover's arms, her eyes radiant with unshed tears.

It was time for Christmas Dinner.

A lot of love, time and effort had gone into its preparation. It was served as a buffet. It was much too hot for the traditional cold climate Christmas dinner. Instead the long trestle table covered in crisp white linen groaned under the weight of the splendid sea food of the Great Barrier Reef waters: lobster, prawns, oysters, scallops, succulent little baby lobsters, the "bugs," a side of Tasmanian smoked salmon and a magnificent whole barramundi that had been steamed in banana leaves, served cold with papaya chilli and coconut salsa. The Christmas turkey had not been left out of the feast. Neither did the lime and macadamia glazed ham which was very, very good. There were salad accompaniments of all kinds, and for dessert instead of the traditional plum pudding refreshing vanilla poached fruit, peaches, pears, nectarines and berries served with sauternes custard and vanilla ice cream.

"I'm full!" Max sat back limply, rotating a hand around his flat stomach.

"Not *full,* darling," Miranda protested. "How vulgar! In my day it was an elegant sufficiency."

"Nothing elegant about that." Max grinned. "That was a blow out!"

"I'm glad you enjoyed it," Gilly smiled encouragingly across the table at the boy. She and Max had really hit it off. Part of the reason was, Max reminded Gilly of a lost loved one. "You have your sister to thank," Gilly pointed out. "Bronte did most of the work."

"And I loved doing it!" Bronte's eyes outshone the precious gem on her finger. There was so much joy in her she wondered she wasn't elevating. "I'm so glad you joined us, Mother."

"Hear, hear!" Max and Steven saluted Miranda with their drinks. Even Gilly smiled benignly. Miranda had appeared on their doorstep saying she was staying a whole week.

"I owed it to you," Miranda said with a virtuous expression. "I put you children through a terrible time, though I risked a lot myself." She looked up bravely with unexpected tears in her eyes. "I haven't been much of a mother."

"Darn right!" Gilly drawled sotto voce.

"Well…" Miranda tried to ignore Gilly—not an easy thing to do—picking up her confession. "I'm ashamed I was so difficult over Nat, Bronte, when Steven here is so obviously the man to make you gloriously happy. Forgive me for that.''

Bronte reached across the dining room table beautifully set with its Christmas decorations to squeeze her mother's hand. ''I'm happy enough to forgive anyone *anything!*'' she said.

''Not *me*,'' Max announced bluntly. ''I'm never going to forgive my father. I'm not going home, either. I'm staying here if you'll let me, Mum. It's okay with the family which of course includes Steven.'' He looked around the smiling, supportive faces. ''We've talked about it. There'll be some exciting things going on in the New Year I have to be part of. Steven's already checked out a good school. I can get in. I'm not going to take any more of that man's abuse. I'm expecting you to go into bat for me, Mum. I'm not ever going back, I swear.''

Miranda, suddenly pale as paper, took a big gulp of her wine. ''The fact is…'' She paused and looked at each of them in turn, her beautiful eyes soulful and as round as saucers. ''The fact is…''

''Well?'' Max's boyish voice cracked.

Miranda waved her elegant, perfectly manicured hands in the air. She really was an awesomely beautiful woman. ''Don't make me nervous, Max. The fact is…''

''Let me help you, my dear,'' Gilly intervened with a lick of sarcasm. ''Carl Brandt mightn't be Max's father at all. It could very well have been my poor nephew, Ross. Is that right, Miranda? I for one won't be particularly surprised.''

Bronte made a quick clutch at Steven's arm as if for support, staring at her mother with astounded eyes. ''Is this true?''

''Why the hell not!'' Gilly remarked dryly.

Max jumped up from his chair and went to his mother, kneeling beside her. ''Say yes! Say yes,'' he begged. ''It's the one thing I want to hear most in this world. Carl Brandt *isn't* my father.''

Miranda propped up her head with her hand. ''Please don't

yell at me, darling. I just have to take a minute or two… At the beginning I wasn't sure,'' she said tremulously.

"You're such a liar, Miranda,'' Gilly scoffed. "Come clean. Then maybe your children can forgive you.''

"What do you want me to say, Gilly?'' Miranda sat bolt upright, looking flushed and very sorry for herself.

"That you've lived a lie for the past fifteen years. Who knows why. The money, I suppose. You always had to have it.''

"Miranda, it *is* time to put everything straight,'' Steven advised her gently, clasping Bronte's hand firmly in his. "No matter what you've done, your children will stand by you. We'll *all* stand by you while you free yourself of Brandt.''

"You've been so good to me already, Steven.'' Miranda batted her long eyelashes at this wonderfully handsome and charming young man. "Okay so I ran away from my marriage to Ross. I abandoned Bronte. When I realized I was pregnant I wasn't sure who the father was.''

Gilly gave a wry grunt. "You're not convincing me any, but you somehow convinced Brandt he was the father. That must have taken some doing. But you always were a great actress. I seem to be the only one who could read your mind.''

"Forgive me.'' Miranda bent her head like a supplicant desperately in need of their pity. "It didn't take me long to work it out. Of course Max is Ross's child—he's like him, haven't you noticed?—but I couldn't possibly have told Carl. I mean it wouldn't have been *safe!* He'd have killed me.''

"Instead he nearly killed me.'' Max rose slowly to his feet. "I used to joke about Brandt not being my father, but this is really weird. You *stayed* with the bastard, Mum. Why didn't you get out with some self-respect?''

"She wanted to be sure of the money?'' suggested Gilly.

"I had to, Max.'' Miranda looked up at her young son, pleading for his understanding if she couldn't get it from anyone else. "He was my husband.''

"Gosh, that didn't stop you from leaving Ross," Gilly piped up.

Miranda opened her lovely mouth to retort. Closed it at the expression in Gilly's snapping black eyes.

"Hey, we really are brother and sister!" Max brightened miraculously. He looked across at Bronte, whooping with joy. "So when are you going to tell him, Mum?"

"What and give up what he owes you? Owes *me!*" Miranda cried, sounding like she was about to hyperventilate. "I'm looking for a big settlement. There's no need for him to know you're not his son, Maxie," she cajoled. "You stand to inherit a fortune one day. He suffers from very high cholesterol, you know. He could pop off just like that!"

"Wouldn't that be awful," Gilly said, with quiet disgust. "On the other hand, you suffer from a very high level of greed, Miranda. No, you're going to come clean. Save your soul. You never know, it might feel good."

"You don't tell him, Mum. I will," Max said, plonking down beside his sister and picking up a chocolate.

"So will I," Bronte said, a determined tilt of her chin.

"Count me in," Steven added.

"You know what *I'm* likely to do, Miranda," Gilly said. "Carl Brandt is a bad, bad man. Count yourself lucky you got away from him."

"It's just that…" Miranda plucked at her magnificent pearls, obviously seeing a fortune slipping away when it should have been hers.

Gilly as the most senior member of the family spoke for all of them. "You won't fail us, Miranda. Not *this* time."

To her credit Miranda didn't.

For the rest at that Christmas table, a blissfully happy Bronte and Steven, a liberated Max and a reenergised Gilly it was the start of a wonderful year. It marked the return of Oriole Plantation to all its former glory and so much more. Bronte and Steven celebrated their fairy tale wedding there, making full use of the gloriously landscaped grounds designed by that master, Leo Marsdon, among the guests, and the newly built banquet hall. Their wedding—guests couldn't stop gushing for months about how marvellous it was—and this started what was to become a custom for local brides, securing Oriole for their wedding venue before they did anything else. The imagination could scarcely picture a more beautiful place. All those ponds and lakes, the playing fountains, so refreshing in the heat!

Even the McAllister ancestors were happy.

TO WIN HIS HEART by Rebecca Winters

(The Husband Fund)

Bubbly blonde heiress Olivia Duchess is attracted to gorgeous Frenchman Luc de Falcon, and he's attracted to her – but his famous racing driver brother is infatuated with her. Luc is an honourable man, but Olivia has the Husband Fund at her disposal, and is determined to win his heart...

THE MONTE CARLO PROPOSAL by Lucy Gordon

Multimillionaire Jack Bullen has a proposal for Della Martin: pose as his girlfriend in Monte Carlo so he can avoid an unwanted marriage. Della agrees, only to find that kissing and flirting with Jack when it's all 'pretend' is hard. She wants it for real...

THE LAST-MINUTE MARRIAGE by Marion Lennox

(Contract Brides)

Peta and Marcus had a wonderful wedding – but it's a sham. Theirs is a marriage of convenience. Yet Marcus is showering his bride with gifts and offering a life of luxury – but Peta wants *Marcus* not money...

THE CATTLEMAN'S ENGLISH ROSE by Barbara Hannay

(Southern Cross)

An Outback cattle station is the last place Charity Denham thought she'd end up searching for her brother – she won't leave until she finds him. Kane McKinnon lives for the Outback, but he harbours a secret – one that Charity is close to discovering...

On sale 3rd December 2004

Christmas is a time for miracles...

Christmas Deliveries

Caroline Anderson   Marion Lennox

Sarah Morgan

On sale 3rd December 2004

Available at most branches of WHSmith, Tesco, ASDA, Martins, Borders, Eason, Sainsbury's and all good paperback bookshops.

WE VALUE YOUR OPINION!

YOUR CHANCE TO WIN A ONE YEAR SUPPLY OF YOUR FAVOURITE BOOKS.

If you are a regular UK reader of Mills & Boon® Tender Romance™ and have always wanted to share your thoughts on the books you read—here's your chance:

Join the Reader Panel today!

This is your opportunity to let us know exactly what you think of the books you love.

And there's another great reason to join:

Each month, all members of the Reader Panel have a chance of winning four of their favourite Mills & Boon romance books EVERY month for a whole year!

If you would like to be considered for the Reader Panel, please complete and return the following application. Unfortunately, as we have limited spaces, we cannot guarantee that everyone will be selected.

Name: _____

Address: _____

_____ Post Code: _____

Home Telephone: _____ Email Address: _____

Where do you normally get your Mills & Boon Tender Romance books (please tick one of the following)?

Shops   ❑   Library/Borrowed   ❑

Reader Service™ ❑ If so, please give us your subscription no. _____

Please indicate which age group you are in:

16 – 24   ❑   25 – 34   ❑

35 – 49   ❑   50 – 64   ❑   65 +   ❑

If you would like to apply by telephone, please call our friendly Customer Relations line on **020 8288 2886**, or get in touch by email to readerpanel@hmb.co.uk

Don't delay, apply to join the Reader Panel today and help ensure the range and quality of the books you enjoy.

Send your application to:

**The Reader Service, Reader Panel Questionnaire,
FREEPOST NAT1098, Richmond, TW9 1BR**

If you do not wish to receive any additional marketing material from us, please contact the Data Manager at the address above.

FREE

4 BOOKS AND A SURPRISE GIFT!

We would like to take this opportunity to thank you for reading this Mills & Boon® book by offering you the chance to take FOUR more specially selected titles from the Tender Romance™ series absolutely FREE! We're also making this offer to introduce you to the benefits of the Reader Service™—

- ★ **FREE home delivery**
- ★ **FREE gifts and competitions**
- ★ **FREE monthly Newsletter**
- ★ **Books available before they're in the shops**
- ★ **Exclusive Reader Service offers**

Accepting these FREE books and gift places you under no obligation to buy; you may cancel at any time, even after receiving your free shipment. Simply complete your details below and return the entire page to the address below. You don't even need a stamp!

YES! Please send me 4 free Tender Romance books and a surprise gift. I understand that unless you hear from me, I will receive 6 superb new titles every month for just £2.69 each, postage and packing free. I am under no obligation to purchase any books and may cancel my subscription at any time. The free books and gift will be mine to keep in any case.

N4ZEE

Ms/Mrs/Miss/Mr...Initials ....
                                                              BLOCK CAPITALS PLEASE
Surname ....

Address ....

....

....Postcode ....

Send this whole page to:

The Reader Service, FREEPOST CN81, Croydon, CR9 3WZ